THE EXIT MACHINE

Produced under the *'nom de plume'* (pen name) Leo Arland

Fourth Edition 2013

Disclaimer

THE EXIT MACHINE

(A Dark Comedy Concerning the Office Romances and Internal Politics of a Euthanasia Centre, Set in a World where Assisted Suicide and Euthanasia is No Longer a Matter of Choice)

Isaiah 5:20a
"Woe unto them that call evil good and good evil; who mistake darkness for light and light for darkness"

Thought Starter
Mass murder is easy to organize once you know how

Leo Arland

ISBN: 978-1-907910-09-8

This document was: -

First compiled from June-August 2009

Released onto the Internet in December 2010

Re-titled, January 2011

Revised, February-March 2011

Prepared for publication in book form, April 2011

Further revised September- November 2011

Second *'Test'* Edition Released for local Distribution December 2011

Third Edition Released for International Distribution, August 2012

Contents

Dedication

This book is dedicated to the Russian writer Alexander Solzhenitsyn (1918-2008) who challenged a previous age of inhumanity and provided a role model for the writer.

Also to the American Psychologist Philip Zimbardo whose book *'The Lucifer Effect: How Good People Turn Evil'* proved a major inspiration. His permission to use his name in this dedication is gratefully acknowledged.

It is also dedicated to the millions who may yet perish in the age of dehumanisation that is already beginning to engulf the Western World.

Finally, to the *'New Atheists'* like Richard Dawkins, Christopher Dennett, Anthony Grayling and to all advocates of *'assisted suicide'* and *'euthanasia'* so they can see the kind of society they've been helping to build.

Preface

'The Exit Machine' originated while I was engaged in professional work amongst disabled people. As more and more pro-euthanasia propaganda was being churned out by the media I looked at this group of extremely vulnerable individuals and thought how easily they could become targets. It was this realization that drove me to write this story. A visit to Auschwitz Birkenau (made on Friday 7th October 2011) drove home to me the dreadful consequences that are likely to arise should euthanasia ever be legalised and become 'acceptable' in everyday society. To me that hellish place not only testified to a terrible past, but also warned of an equally terrible future. In the Western World we are in serious danger of seeing the birth of a mass extermination society. As Auschwitz itself demonstrated, murder on an industrial scale can be extremely easy to organize, once the will and the resources are present.

Both chapters were first written on Saturday 8th August 2009 whilst travelling by train to Dawlish for a fortnight's holiday with my wife. During this period of high creativity I could almost hear the voice of Kenny speaking and the plot began to unfold. It examines (in story form) the consequences likely to ensue from any legalisation of assisted suicide. (This had been a much discussed topic in the media shortly before our holiday.) Word processing commenced on Tuesday, 2nd March 2010 when 'assisted dying' was once more hitting the headlines. Quite deliberately, it follows an Alan Bennett 'Talking Heads' format, giving it an immediate presence. Kenny's voice, with its mixed accent, rings out throughout the book, talking as if he really is addressing a 'live' audience on a radio or TV set. In that capacity, he unwittingly acts as a 'stand up comedian' of death.

Some minor additions were made in April-May 2011, after hearing of secondary school pupils being taught about euthanasia through a controversial video in which an 'assisted suicide' campaigner was promoting his cause. On hearing of such developments I commented to my wife, "We are nearer to the age of Kenny than even I first thought.' Final additions were made in early March 2012 and August 2013.

Introduction

Imagine a world without compassion, mercy or kindness, a world where involuntary euthanasia, *'mercy killing'* and assisted suicide have become the norm – where *'the banality of evil'* has triumphed. This is the world of 'The Exit Machine' as told from the often confused and self-aggrandising viewpoint of Kenny, its main character who (with next to no scruples) works as *'a minor functionary'* for *'The Dignity Dispatch Service.'* It consists of two chapters, each relating a dystopian monologue; *'The Dignity Room'* and *'The Dignity Suite'* explore the varied personalities, doomed romances and office politics of Kenny's place of work. Laced with a heavy dose of dark comedy *'The Exit Machine'* provides a narrative that can make readers both laugh and cry. In ironic yet searing ways it portrays the long-term consequences most likely to ensue from any legislation favouring assisted suicide and euthanasia. To read this book is to have one's view of present-day society challenged and to risk being shaken to the very core. The reader will shed all delusions concerning the innate goodness of human nature, gaining a glimpse into what could easily become a terrible tomorrow.

'The Exit Machine' is one of those dystopian stories which follow the literary traditions of George Orwell's *'1984'* and Margaret Atwood's *'The Handmaid's tale.'* It's written in the conviction that cultural developments (from the 1960's onwards) may well have been laying the foundations for a mass extermination society. Although a dystopian fiction, *'The Exit Machine'* does hope to make a positive contribution to the *'euthanasia'* and *'legalisation of assisted suicide'* debates. A brief *'Afterward'* raises awkward questions concerning legally assisted suicide, i.e. will its acceptance encourage that same unquestioning stance that led directly to the carrying out of euthanasia in the Nazi State?

Behind *'The Exit Machine'* lies the assumption that Western Civilization (in the second decade of the twenty-first century) appears to be suffering from a growing mental and moral derangement. Crimes against humanity may well become increasingly acceptable should social, economic and political conditions continue to deteriorate. A consensus to casually accept the mass murder of those deemed '*a burden on society*' could develop very quickly. The speed at which Same Sex Marriages has become a 'normalised' feature of everyday life could well be matched by an equally speedy '*normalisation*' of euthanasia. Should this take place then we really are on the way to the kind of society portrayed in '*The Exit Machine.*' The mass murder of millions could gather apace and take on its own dreadful momentum.

X

CHAPTER 1: THE DIGNITY ROOM

The setting is an untidy bedsit a few decades in the future. An unkempt bed is noticeable in the background whilst a couple of stale coffee cups and an empty lager can stand cluttering a neighbouring chest of drawers. Nearby, a slim box like recorder lies on a faded dresser, a thin red wire attaching it to a microphone. A man in his mid-fifties, complete with beer belly and podgy face enters the room, casually dressed in an off-white T-shirt and cream trousers. He's just placed an open can of lager on the dresser and is passively observing himself as he combs his receding hair. His friends know him as an amiable, easy-to-get-along with character. He has an ingratiating accent which somehow manages to mix North and South Eastern traits, hinting that he may have worked in a variety of places throughout the country. He likes a good gossip, sometimes emphasising a point with a smile, a shrug of the shoulders or a look of exasperation. He now turns to the recorder, pressing a few keys, and then lightly tapping the microphone. A crisp female voice breaks the silence:

"Please give your full name."

"Kenny English."

"Date of birth?"

"12th September 2001."

"Place of birth?"

"Swindon."

"Password?"

"Harriet 1366613."

"Programme?"

"Personalised Resource Reflective Confessional Programme."

"Draft?"

"Unedited."

"Code?"

"HR1XBEA"

"What voice programme do you wish the interviewer to use."

"Simulated female SESAB3."

"Do you wish to proceed?"

"Yes."

"Are you sure?"

"Yes!"

"Are you absolutely sure?"

"Yes!!!"

"Please proceed, speaking clearly and slowly into the microphone. The programme will commence in precisely five seconds: five, four, three, two, one, zero. This programme is now operative. Please commence."

With a raising of his eyebrows Kenny leans closer to the microphone, brushing aside a pale green plate containing the remains of a half eaten sandwich. Lying atop the dresser's oval mirror what looks like a very dead fly imperceptibly raises its head, watching Kenny – a Nano Bug, secretly planted to monitor his every move.

'ello mah name's Kenneth – or *'Kenny'* t' mah mates – yer can call me *'Kenny.'* At work it's more formal; it's *'Senior Dignity Care Officer, Grade Three.'* The idea – so Management say – is to keep an 'ealthy *'psychological distance'* between us and our work. Like me, you may think it's a load of ole rubbish – but that's what them experts from the Milgram Memorial Institute made a point o' tellin' us when we 'ad 'em on a special visit. I much prefer a more informal approach but in mah job you don't ask any questions. Those that do don't last – they disappear in a puff o' smoke so to speak, ahem!'

'Want to know more about my line of work?'

Well, by trainin' I'm a male psychiatric nurse (please don't say 'it could be worse'). I used to work in cheerful places like Broadmoor 'n' Rampton when they were open. You met some right characters there. Did some time workin' in prisons too – the prison system was far bigger then. I don't mind sayin' I was quite popular with both the staff and the inmates – was always known for a light touch, 'specially with the ladies. I'd better say no more – it could compromise professional integrity, ahem. Well, the government 'ad to do something about it – I mean the size o' the Care System – 'specially when the Global Economy went belly-up an' money started runnin' out. A cost effective way 'ad to be found to deal wi' those 'oo were *'deemed to be a burden on society,'* Well, it all made sense dint it? A way was found and yer know what it was so I needn't say more.

Well, before I was recruited, I was one o' the several million unemployed – that was when a person was permitted to be unemployed for more than three months. I was told (in no uncertain terms) by this jumped-up clerk to apply for this new post with the *'The Dignity Care Service'* – as it was known then – if not, I'd 'ave to face 'avin' me benefit cut. (This was just before they computerised the benefit system.) What else could I do? I was just goin' through a messy divorce an' was bein' pushed for maintenance by the ex for 'er kids. I was in debt and faced eviction for non-payment of rent. It was either take the job or go on the streets. Back then you used to see a lot of beggars hangin' around – but not now, that's one problem the 'New World' authorities 'ave sorted out – with a little 'elp from the likes of me of course!

Anyway, I went for the interview with travel costs thankfully paid for by *'The Job Finder Agency.'* I soon discovered that not only were the pay rates double what I were used to but they even 'ad a scheme to 'elp pay off mah debts! A battery of aptitude tests confirmed that a person with mah background and psychological profile would be exceptionally well suited for the job they 'ad 'in mind. Well, it was an offer too good to miss; wouldn't you 'ave accepted it in mah circumstances? The odd thing was that when I told mah Bank (it were called *'Barclays, Lloyds and West'* back then – the time when we still 'ad paper money though it were being phased out) that I were startin' work with the *'Dignity Care Service'* (now known as *the 'Dignity Dispatch Service'* or *'DDS'*) they stopped pesterin' me about that deficit! I got called *'Sir'* by the Manager – an' 'e even offered me another loan! I turned 'im down – I never did trust banks – I remember 'ow they ruined dad's business when I were a kid; that were just after the crash of '08. Dad never got over it – an' he 'n' mum were divorced within a couple o' years. There were a lot o' rows over property 'n' child visitation rights. It were all a bit of a mess.

Another benefit (an' a huge relief to me) was the payments to the *'ex'* got sorted out by the DDS and' a visit from *'Social Amendment Agency'* (in mah younger days they used to be called *'The Police.'*) The DDS always looks after its own. Its aim is t' make the 'crew' (that's what we're called) 'appy. Nowadays, I don't bother wi' marriage. Once was enough – an' relationships are now, shall we say, very much *'in-house.'* It was good to be free again an' I enjoyed 'avin' a bit o' respect although I used to get funny looks from mah mates when I mentioned mah line o' work. Now we're advised by Management to say that we're in – *'the life enhancement industry.'* That's a nifty term, ain't it? Very positive soundin' darn't yer think?

'You wanna know about my present work?'

Well, I came up here eight years ago after I'd finished workin' for the Dignity *'humane prison closure'* scheme. That was all very *'hush, hush'* at the time. Assisted suicide had just been legalised and, thanks to an effective publicity campaign, the idea of removin' those deemed *'a burden on society'* was in the air. 'owever, success couldn't be guaranteed – there were always them 'Human Rights' lawyers 'oo could kick-up a right fuss. Unlike today, *'Mercy Dispatching'* wasn't viewed as bein' normal. People still 'ad questions about it. I remember 'em arguin' 'ammer an tongs about it on *'Querry Time'* and other such programmes, (run by the old BBC before its merger with *'Global Cloud Communications Unlimited.'*)

'How did we start?'

It was with the child killers first, the really nasty ones – we made sure they 'ad no relatives to cause a fuss an' we went on from there. With this sort o' thing it was judged best to start with obvious hate figures, 'to test the waters' so to speak. The first 'clinical' trials were a bit grim with some twitching and convulsing but we improved the quality o' the drugs up to 'international termination standards' an' things got much better. One of the biggest changes – an' it 'elped us a lot – was when injections were given by robotic machines – computerised gizmos with *'fail safes'* thrown in too. It 'elped to retain that sense of *'professional detachment'* – a definite *'must'* for this job. It's amazin' 'ow much these machines streamlined everythin' – it all got so much easier – very slick, very efficient. *'Dispatchin''* was just in a day's work.

'Was there any fuss?'

Nah! Not really. Some lawyers did cause a spot o bother but they were next on the dispatch list. I like it, get rid of the criminals an' then their defence lawyers! Great eh? Never did 'ave much time for 'em – especially after the *'ex'* got 'er solicitor to screw me for every last penny. After the prisons it became fairly easy to arrange for the *'demographic reallocation'* of 'ospitals an' nursin' homes. Relatives were so grateful to be relieved of the trouble of administering the *'Dignity Dose'* themselves. Back then Opinion Polls showed that we enjoyed a lot of public support.

'How did I come up here?'

Easy, I did mah work so well that promotion came fast. When the right post came up here, I applied, 'ad a good interview and was accepted as Senior Dignity Care Officer, Grade Three. This was a big step up for me as I'd been workin' to Grade One Assistant Level before that. Soon a Grade Four Supervisor's job will be goin' an' I think I'll apply fer it. It should be a meal ticket to the middle classes – I bet the *'ex'* is sorry that she ever chucked me out.

'Do you foresee any problems in your work?'

Well, the only problem I can foresee is with the week-long residential course when we're tested to see if we can 'andle the paperwork. I'm dyslexic yer see but fortunately that's a *'non-terminatory condition.'* Apologies for the jargon but my line o' work is full of it and it's always changing,' an' even at my lowly rank you 'ave to learn it. What used to be called *'Mercy Killing'* is now known as *'Happy Dispatching'* or 'HD' for short. (Personally, I prefer to use the one word *'Dispatching'* cos, it neatly sums up what we do.) The phrase *'Permanent Respiting'* began to get bandied about but Management soon put a stop to it – sayin' it was a bit too clumsy. I disagree – for me it 'ad an air of 'elpfulness about it – relievin' the burden for carers, so to speak. Well Management said *'No'* 'n' that was that. There was even talk of our job title changin' to *Blissful Awakening Agent'* – but that was goin' a little too far, even for the Public Relations Department. I think it was their idea of a joke – or at least I 'ope it was!

'What are your duties?'

Well, I'm comin' onto that. I work in a *'Dignity Dispatch Unit.'* (They used to be called *'Mercy Care Units'* or *'MCU's,'* now they're *'DDU's.'*) It all 'appens in this one room – *'The Dignity Room,'* although we staff like to call it the *'The Dispatch 'atch'* – it does 'elp to 'ave a sense of humour in our line o' work. Across the corridor are a couple of other rooms – one where we keep the *'stiffs'* – whoops! I mean the *'dispatchees'* and one where we take our break. One thing you nearly always see clutterin' up the corridor outside are the trolleys. They're all 'angin about, just waitin' there, carryin' soon to be dispatched or already safely dispatched 'uman cargo. There's a very simple colour scheme – trolleys covered in green paper sheets mean they're goods awaitin' dispatch; those in red are the goods that have already been dispatched. *'Red'* Trolleys get taken to *'The House of Bliss'* or what used to be called *'The Morgue.'* (It's funny how words keep on changin'.) The simple colour scheme really 'elps the migrant workers – 'specially those with a poor grasp of English. Even they can't go wrong with it – at least I 'ope not!

'The room we work in?'

To be frank, it's a bit on the dingy side, but it's where our business gets done. The paint's a dirty grey colour and its beginnin' to peel off the walls. We've been on at Management for months now to give us a new coat o' paint, but still nothin' gets done. We keep bein' told, *'It's proceeding down official channels',* whatever that means. You know what *'The National Life Service'* bureaucracy is like. I did arrange for vases of flowers to brighten things up a little, but I still think we could do more – an' it grates on me that our workroom overlooks the rubbish area in the inner courtyard. It makes us feel a bit shut away an' secluded an' a bit snubbed too, if truth be told. I suppose it's all done in such borin' surroundings so as not to attract unwanted attention.

Despite the 'igh scores in Opinion Polls an' the big Government awards, Senior Management still like to remain 'discreet.' Most of 'em can still remember the days when *'Care'* was all about the preservation of life. (How expensive that was!) Whether things ll change when our Euro Group Chairman, Dr Galton retires to get 'is Peerage remains to be seen. The fact that 'e recently won a Nobel Prize for *'services rendered to Human Sustainability'* should open things up a bit make it all more acceptable 'n' palatable to the wider public. But, as it stands just now, men of 'is generation still tend to be quiet 'n' cautious. Their idea was to let it all *'bed in'* slowly. Still, when all's said 'n' done we definitely need somethin' better than these grotty Victorian premises.

'You want to know more about my daily routine?'

Hmm! T' understand it you must see that we're part of a wider process. In their wisdom Management 'ave broken it down into what they call *'a logical dispatch flow.'* The idea is t' ensure a quick entrance an' a quick exit for our goods. The *'service consumer'* or what we call the *'dispatchee'* is told (if they're the least bit likely t' kick-up a fuss) that they've got to 'ave an emergency operation or some kind of 'special treatment'. (That's a good one in't it – *'special treatment'* eh? Funny eh?) Then they're dosed with a heavy anaesthetic and a green (not a white label) is attached to their wrist. This contains details o' their name, age 'n' address. Patients with different labels are wheeled out at the same time, but the one with the white wrist band goes for genuine treatment, while the one wearin' the green wrist band comes to us. Once Management tried to play around with black wrist labels – but that was seen to 'ave negative connotations. Apparently, the jumped up officials at *'The Ethnic Relations Council'* criticised them for *'negative racial stereotyping'* and so we kept to the green wrist bands even though they contrasted less well with the white ones. Most dispatchees come from the 'ospital but we do get the odd one from the local police station – usually a piece of *'street trash'* they've just picked up and want to get rid of. We 'ave strict instructions not to report on any bruises we may find on their bodies. The police (Oh I mean *The Social Amendment Agency'*) are rather sensitive about their reputation. Sometimes they administer the anaesthetic – but don't ask me 'ow –

they never seem to make a good job of it. Well, quite a lot of their time, their dispatchees comes round just as we're about to send 'im (or 'er) to a better life. That can be a bit awkward. We don't get many such cases these days – most criminals were cleared out years ago. Nowadays, the police are concerned with monitoring our internal security an' guardin' our borders against the unwashed masses wantin' to flood in from the southern regions. I aven't a clue as to why they want to come; things are bad enough 'ere. Personally, I blame all this on climate change an' the internal tribal wars they keep 'avin'. There's always famine in the south too – tragic really – it never seems t' get any better.

'What's your part in the dispatching process?'

Well all that 'appens is that when a bell rings a dispatchee is left outside our door. Before wheelin' 'im or 'er in, we carefully check that both the trolley sheets and the *'dispatchee'* wrist band are coloured green and personal ID is crosschecked too. We then wheel 'em into the Dignity Room for intermediate processin'. Records are again cross checked to see if the serial numbers match. The arm is then attached to *'The Exit Machine'* and some buttons are pressed. An automated injection goes in an' within minutes the Dispatche (properly known as the *'Service Consumer'*) 'as gone to 'appy land. Thanks to better technology we can use *'The Exit Machine'* to check the dispatchee's pulse an' brain activity. Only when all such activity ceases do we press the buttons to withdraw the instruments. It's all over in five minutes. There are three Exit Machines in our room though usually only two are in operation at any one time. (The third one comes *'on line'* busy times.) The advantage for us is that we've no physical contact with the cargo. This does make things a lot easier. But I wish they weren't painted in black, I mean that's a little too gothic! Out of consideration the dispatchee's head is covered in a green paper bag. Psychologists from the Milgram Institute thought it would make our work easier. 'owever, just the other week it was embarrassin' to find that some o' the bags 'ad the name of our local supermarket *'Morco'* printed in gold lettering all over 'em! (This was durin' the last inflow when all of our usual bags 'ad run out.) There was a right fuss an' things got quickly sorted out after Management sent round a memo tellin' us that their use *'wasn't in accordance with the dignity and standing of our profession.'* 'owever, after all this cafuffle I decided to do mah shopping elsewhere. I like to keep mah work an' leisure life separate – it's easier that way. Oh, an' the bags were phased out anyway. After this latest 'run' we're usin' some sort of eco-friendly material just draped over the face. Why Management 'adn't thought o' this before I'll never know.

'What happens next?'

Once the dispatchee is disconnected we wheel 'em out, buzz the porter staff and then resume our work on the next batch. The only thing we 'ave to do is to place a red sheet over the trolley so the porters can wheel 'em to the *'The House of Bliss.'* As I said earlier most of the porters can't speak much English; 'ospital management like it that way because they're less likely t' *'give voice'* shall we say if things ain't goin as smooth as they ought to (which can 'appen from time t' time 'cos we're only 'uman after all, ain't we?) The 'ospital also 'angs onto their work permits which gives 'em a further 'old. A Doctor may do a *'spot check'* to see we've done our job properly but they 'ardly 'ever set foot in our actual *'Dispatch Room'* unless there's any bother. They prefer to keep their distance.

'What are the most satisfying features of this job?'

Beyond the pay I like the steady routine; you know 'oo you are when you press all the right buttons. I also like the feelin' that yer playing a part in reducin' the world's population surplus an' 'elpin' bring about a more sustainable environment for future generations. At mah level there's no fuss or bother wi' the paperwork. Once an assignment's completed all I've to do is record the termination time (even to the minute). Our organization likes to be very precise with its statistics. I 'eard from mah supervisor, that last year there were only one million dispatches – not nearly as large as when we first started out. Back then it just seemed to go on forever – dispatch after dispatch – dizzyin' really. Still, we're well on the way to accomplishin' the official

Brussels target of a 25% reduction in the world's population. In this region of Europa, it means reducin' a population of seventy-five million by some seventeen-and-a-half million – mebbe more if we're allowed to exceed targets – which is nearly always the case. I think in the end we'll knock it down by about twenty million. That way we'll 'ave ensured the survival of the fittest members of all of the world's societies. The idea is to 'elp push along the processes of evolution – all very straightforward when yer think about it. It's all about sustainability yer see – Management always 'ave that at the back of their minds – that's why they're always aimin' t' exceed dispatch targets. The prison population 'as been dispatched, the elderly and sick 'ave been dispatched, unwanted minorities 'ave been dispatched, an' anyone the government 'as branded as an anti-social element 'as been dispatched. Oh, and so 'ave most lawyers (as there's now no crime to speak of), but we're avin' difficulty in achievin' our targets. The Global Authorities are now proposin' tax rebates an' a relief on any debts t' encourage voluntary dispatchin'. Sounds all well an' good but I still don't think they'll get the numbers.

'So what's likely to happen if not enough are being dispatched?'

Well, they'll just 'ave to widen the categories to cover more groups. Already there's talk of *'inclusive dispatching'* (whatever that means) but that's somethin' I'm 'appy ter leave t' Management. They'll let us know more about it as time goes on. My role is just t'get on wi' the job an' ask no questions.

'How many service consumers are dispatched in a typical working day?'

Hmm! that varies – dependin' on whether there's a dispatch campaign goin' on or not. At present we're in a quiet patch an' the authorities 'ave put us on short time until another disposable minority 'as been selected. But usually, allowin' for all the paperwork an' data entry that needs ter be done, we can, at a steady pace, manage six an hour – twelve if the other Exit Machine is in operation. Above that you 'ave to use the reserve machine and then you're talkin' double shifts. Durin' a major wave we 'ave to sleep *'on the job'* so to speak, takin' what naps we can on the camp beds they've provided. When this 'appens things get really cramped and the atmosphere can be... eh, how shall I put it, a little tetchy? During the last wave there was a shortage of trolleys. There was quite a pile-up of cargo outside and some items 'ad to be piled up – one on top of o' the other. It were an 'ot summer and we 'ad to curb the smell with air freshener, which a bit of a nuisance as it always makes me sneeze. We also 'ad ter take extra precautions because some o' the cargos were infectious diseases cases. In the end, the job got done and we received a *'Shipman Certificate of Commendation.'* We even went out *'clubbin'* to celebrate although Management did ask us to wear strong deodorant. Mah Supervisor even made a point o' givin' me a bottle of strong aftershave although I never use the stuff.

'How well does this unit compare with others?'

Oh, we're not a large *'Burden Disposal Unit'* (oh I mean *'DDU'*) like you 'ave in Euro Capital Three (formally London) or other big cities. We're a sub-branch of a branch if yer get mah meanin'. But we do 'ave a bit o' rivalry with a neighbourin' Unit which is also based in an 'ospital. They get through 11 dispatches to every 10 of ours. (Management expect us to know these ratios.) 'owever, our Supervisor pointed out that they 'ave better facilities and are based in an inner city area where there's more problem families to dispatch. (We're now down to the disposable hospital patients and the odd police disposal case.) Unfortunately, Management treat our explanations as excuses and somehow we've got to improve our Dispatch Rate. They're especially sore that this other Unit won a *Termination Efficiency Award'* and a generous bonus to go along with it. So there's a whiff of change in the air – but it's not our fault that our facilities aren't as good as theirs! I mean, just what do they expect? On an 'appier note the efficiency of our record keeping was commended. It's funny 'ow bureaucracy chases you even after you're dead – oh no, what I mean of course is, *'promoted to a place of higher bliss,'* hee-hee!'

'What about the head injury cases?'

Yes, we 'andle 'em but they're really a sideline. At one time they were called *'warm cabbages'* until protests from the Cabbage Growing Association disallowed the use of that term. It used to be the case that if there was no improvement within six months they would be sent for dispatchin'. Now, for budgetary reasons, it's down to three months and there's talk of cuttin' it down to a month 'though I think that's a bit too short; it doesn't allow relatives to adjust. Followin' that mega-speed train crash a few months back we gained twenty-three dispatch cases. When a motorway pile-up 'appened last year we received nine cases. Accidents are – if you like – *'good for business'* so long as they don't 'appen to you of course! With what the government calls our *'current decaying infrastructure'* the accident ratios are gonna increase – stands t' reason don't it? You just 'ave ter look around yer – roads full o' pot 'oles 'n' pavements missin' kerb stones 'an the like. It's a right blimin' mess and it's gonner t' get worse with the latest spending cutbacks. We also benefit whenever the government wants a cull of unwanted migrants. Those 'oo ain't any use end-up here, either pushin' the trolleys or bein' on the trolleys! There's always a stream of 'em. As I said earlier, I don't know why they want to come to this 'umble province of Europa but they still do. Mebbe it's because their governments 'ave less 'umane ways of removin' their liabilities. Over 'ere, it's far more clinical an' efficient. In the Southern Regions they still use machétees would you believe it! Now that's what I call barbaric!

'Do I like the job?'

Course I do!!! It's double the normal pay rates an' there's plenty o' perks. Their Financial Care Service is top class – it got me out o' debt straightaway and shut-up the *'ex'* for good! I also like the banter with mah workmates which I view as another perk – although you 'ave to be careful not to go too far. Nonetheless, mah own brand o' humour does 'elp lighten things up. We also get good media publicity so our position carries a certain status, even though we get the odd funny look now an' again. There are some *'off days'* at times but generally I'm at peace with what I do. I like to think I'm doin' mah bit to 'elp sustain the world's population an' create a more human-friendly environment. At least, unlike the Southern Region, we don't rely on famine to do our work for us. Hmm – you could even say I'm in the business of ecological preservation. Some years ago, there was even talk about re-branding our organization – calling it the *'International Ecological Preservation Corporation.'* But no – some of the *'Greens'* (as they were called) got all upset and the idea was dropped. Pity really – I think it would 'ave cast us in a good light. Those *'Greens'* must 'ave 'ad friends in *'High Places'* – otherwise they would 'ave ended-up on the Trolleys – just like those anarchists did years back. Overall, I'm very 'appy in mah work. Without exaggeration I can say it's mah life. Management know me as *'the positive dispatcher.'*

'Concerning staff relations?'

Among the team it's pretty good. We're all in it together as you might say. Our Supervisor, *('Baldie Eagle'* we call 'im) allows a relaxed atmosphere and we 'ave a laugh about the false fur lined coats 'e likes to buy for 'imself. 'e comes to work on this strange 'ome-made tricycle thing – says 'e makes 'em for environmental reasons. He's into what's called Eco DIY. We say it's to make up for the lack of 'air on 'is head. We also 'ad this shrink from the *'Zimbardo Faculty at the Milgram Memorial Institute'* to 'elp us *'bond'* together as a team. It all involved trudging through the Lake District an' doin' all sorts of activities which reminded me o' the stuff they used to do in that *'Big Brother'* show which I watched as a kid. One geezer 'oo kept on criticisin' everythin' we did was removed from the programme – it was felt that 'e wouldn't fit in with our line o' work. 'e failed to see that our role was not to ask questions but to get on with the job. 'e was so negative that they put 'im into the accounts section which is where 'e belonged. Staff initiative's all very well in the area of operations – but not policy – that's for the ''igh-ups' to decide. It's what's called *'controlled delegation.'* Sorry if I'm spoutin' too much *'management speak'* but it 'elps to use it in our line of business. Knowin' the jargon gets you promotion.

'Are there any problems in staff relations?'

I don't want to be politically incorrect or be branded a *'male chauvinist piglet'* (as the *'ex'* used to call me) but between you 'n' me I think this should be a man's job. I may sound old fashioned but that's mah stated opinion. Women can fuss too much, especially when children are involved. There was one case of an operative 'oo tried ter smuggle a baby 'ome an' it were only through a careful monitorin' o' figures that she was found out. That wasn't our Unit (thank goodness) but it does prove mah point. 'owever, in their wisdom, the *'Ministry of Care'* ('oo still have a big say in the runnin' of things, despite privatization) 'ave decreed that at least one-third of operatives should be female, even though they're far more difficult to recruit. This was in response to a scandal at the 'arringway Unit some while back. The male staff members 'ad engaged in 'orseplay with the 'dear departed' – puttin' cigars in their mouths an' beer glasses on the trolleys – that sort o' thing. I can't remember all the details. Unfortunately some clever so and so took it into their 'ead to take pictures an' didn't they go all round the blinkin Globe! If we still 'ad newspapers an' the BBC the bad publicity would 'ave been worse but, even so, 'eads 'ad ter roll. Those responsible were of course *'trolleyfied'* and the fuss blew over. 'owever, thinkin' it were the best sort of response, (Ah totally disagree) the Directorate felt it right ter *'balance the gender intake of staff.'* So now we 'ave to take on women. Even today the 'arringway Unit still 'as a funny reputation and (unofficially) Management are known to be reluctant to take on staff from there.

'Why do you think things went wrong at Harringway?'

Ummm! Not sure, from what I 'eard on the grapevine, its speciality was pre-teen dispatchin' (it doesn't really 'ave the same status as our work yer know). Their team consisted of a failed social worker (who was leadin' it) an' some o' the less pleasant elements o' society. As part of our staff trainin' we once did a case study which I think was based upon 'arringway an' we 'ad to pick-out all the things that went wrong. It were also emphasised that *The DDS greatly values its high public reputation.'* I think Chairman Galton was a bit worried about 'is peerage. It's odd but we do get a lot of ex social workers in our line o' work. I suppose they get some enjoyment from knockin' off their former clients. More usually, they go off into Management an' make our work more difficult. Psychologists are even worse; they always want us to do these fancy *'motivation'* tests so as t' improve our efficiency. In my 'umble opinion they should be trolleyfied but I suppose they do put across a sort of *'genteel intelligentsia'* type o' feel that lends credibility to our service. They provide us with an air of respectability.

'What contributions does the female staff make to your work?'

Oh, ah, hmm! I get along with women (apart from the *'ex'*) but for me (as someone from a workin' class background) the proper place for 'em is in the kitchen. That's 'ow I were brought up on the Swindon Council Estate. I don't begrudge 'em doin' office administration either – it saves me a lot of 'assle with the paperwork. But the ones you get 'ere are not the types you want to pull – even if you're paralytic. Those 'oo do end-up 'ere always seem to be under some sort of a cloud – like there's somethin' nigglin' at 'em all of the time, if yer catch mah drift.

The first one we 'ad were actually a Doctor an' strike me down, she were great! Surprisin' really ... Harriet Love was 'er name and phoah! Did she 'ave class! Been to an all girls private school an' all that; spoke dead posh! Couldn't work out at first what she were doin' 'ere at all but later I found out that when she was on the 'ospital wards the death rate would mysteriously rise, (particularly among those patients 'oo didn't 'ave relatives to cause a fuss). Sometimes the death rate would treble. This discrepancy were noticed and 'uman Resources 'ad a quiet word with 'er, suggestin' that 'er talents would be better deployed in the DDS. She couldn't argue an' that's 'ow she came onto our patch. She'd been told to lie low for a year or two an' then promotion would come 'er way. At first she was as quiet as a church mouse an' she 'ad that look on 'er face which suggested that she weren't entirely sure whether she were goin' to be put onto the Dispatch List 'erself. I think she also felt that we were a bit beneath 'er, but I switched on mah charm an' 'elped her to get accepted as one o' the team. After about a month she settled down – just took it all in 'er stride. Nothin' ever seemed to phase our 'arriet. It were 'arriet 'oo suggested that we should 'ave flowers on the window sill. She really took to 'er work an' at one point our dispatch rate even exceeded that of our rivals. We got a commendation from Management for that. Yeah! Great, eh! We got on like an 'ouse on fire 'arriet n me – I often used to make 'er laff. But she 'ad one odd thing about 'er – an obsession with cleanliness; everythin' 'ad to be 'just so' (she would also spend much of 'er break in the shower.) She often told us that she viewed our work as a kind of *'cleansing.'* Sadly, she were too good to stay with the likes of us. Management saw 'er potential and, after about eighteen months she were promoted, first to Human Resources (or HR) and then as Senior Advisor to the Pensioner Reduction Quango – yer know – one o' those obscure bodies supposed ter guide government policy regardin' the elderly. Until a couple o' years ago she used to send us one of 'er effusive *'Winterval Cards'* – in one of these she told us 'ow, unlike other Management, she would spend at least two hours a week on Dispatch Operations. She viewed it as some form of relaxation therapy. Apparently 'er *'hands on'* approach was much appreciated. Ah Harriet! She 'ad class, an' should go far in 'er career. I would like there to have been somethin' between us – but she could never 'ave stood mah untidy ways – would 'ave quickly recommended me for cleansing – hee-hee. Still, I used to raise a smile on 'er face. She once said I were 'er *'darling mentor.'* An' ter this day I've a sentimental soft spot for 'er. I'd love ter know 'ow she were gettin' on!

'After Harriet?'

We got lumbered with Deidre. With most girls I can raise a laugh – but not Deidre. She'd done funny things at a Child Containment Centre (they used to be called Nurseries). It was so serious that even Management didn't know – only the *'big chief'* Dr Galton 'imself – or so it was said. As with 'arriet, the DDS stepped in and gave our Deidre a choice – either work for them or become a *'service user.'* They also promised 'er free access to certain substances she 'ad an addiction to. The result was that everyone got what they wanted;

Management a new Exit Operative, Deidre 'er substances and we got an extra pair of hands as a new wave were comin' in. At first she were a little shy about usin' the Exit Machine but when I jokingly said, *'It's either the injection you like to use or it's one you don't!'* she got on with 'er work competently enough. 'owever, she's not allowed near any computers – don't know why but must have been somethin' to do with what went wrong in 'er previous job.

Deidre gets the job done quickly enough but she's not exactly the most communicative of souls. In exchange for no fuss bein' made about 'er 'abits or past misdemeanours she 'ad to undergo forced sterilisation. That can 'ave a funny effect upon women. Mah own 'ex' 'ad it when she went over 'er recomended limit of two children – 'oo, so she said, were not by me! Overall, I'd say Deidre were a competent if not an outstanding operative; but I can't ever see 'er goin on t' 'igher things like 'arriet – now she were the one!'

'How close are relationships with other departments?'

Not much ter say really; we don't exactly mix with 'em. The Doctors occasionally come in (with our Supervisor) to check over some of the *'due to be dispatched'* cases to see whether any organs can be 'arvested. If so, they sign a *'body investment form'* n 'ave em wheeled away an' we're still allowed to keep 'em on our figures. Anythin' that 'elps with our *'exit data,'* so t' speak, is a bonus to us. Senior Management may make a flying visit but that's all. The Docs are always knackered – I've never seen a bright faced one yet! This is because, quite sensibly, Management only deploy them to us at the end o' one of their shifts – when they really can't do anything else. Mind you, the older Doctors are always grim-faced an' never say a word. I don't think some of 'em quite approve of our work. They think they're way above us, all 'high an' mighty' they are. That's typical.

Mind you, the surgeons find us useful. They can bury their mistakes with us. This is because any deaths can be recorded on our records instead of theirs. This makes both our performance and theirs look a whole lot better. I always know a surgeon wants our 'elp when 'e or she winks at us in the corridor or sends a student requesting our assistance with an awkward problem. We've been gettin' an increase of *'cargo transfers'* of late. This must be due to the declinin' quality of 'ealth care. I also get the impression that surgeons like to try out new techniques on their patients. There's one 'oo is nicknamed *'slasher.'* If you go to 'im you risk coming out with important parts missin'. But there's another 'oo's worse! If you go in with one 'ead yer risk comin' out with two! Just jokin, I 'ope!

'Are we accepted by other staff?'

'ard to say, when I first came 'ere I got some strange sideways looks from the nursin' staff an' over'eard someone mutter, *There goes a member of the Dignity Death Squad,'* which I thought were a bit off. In response Management arranged fer us t' eat alone in the small room I've told yer about. They even lay tea an' biscuits on fer us – the ones wi' the nice jam centres. They say it's a bonus because, unlike other Care Staff, we 'ave to do our own cleanin', 'though we have the odd porter ter wash the floors. So we're pretty isolated really. To relieve this we meet with other teams for trainin' or to be briefed if a 'new wave' is about to come in. Much o' the time is spent *'talkin' shop'* an' *'learnin' best practice'* from Gold Star Units (we're only Bronze Star). Afterwards, we go *'clubbin'* or even to the Cinema or Theatre to see a new porno production. Management 'ave even set-up a Dating Agency to reduce the risk of our work causin' relationship problems. I don't use it mahself 'cause yer tend to get those *'Deidre types'* 'oo end-up bein' more trouble than they're worth. Also there's a shortage of women in our line o' work so they've 'ad to allow women from the Security Services to apply. The problem is that some of 'em 'ave 'ad obligatory testosterone therapy to make 'em more efficient in their job an' this 'ardly makes 'em an attractive proposition! Maybe when I get older I may change mah mind, but for now I'm too busy 'avin' a good time to bother with a long lastin' relationship. In mah experience they tend t' cause nothin' but trouble.

'Ever had any major problems at work?'

On the 'ole things run pretty smoothly, even though the strain can show through when a *'big wave'* is on. We sometimes get too many consignments all at once an' they can cause a major pile-up in the corridor outside. Come to think of it, there was just one odd incident that caused a little bother. It 'appened when 'arriet 'ad just started. We 'ad this really old lady – 110 she was, the oldest we've ever 'ad. She'd been kept 'idden by 'er family until the government decided to clear-up the disposable minorities. For some reason, the earlier anaesthetic 'adn't taken 'old (maybe it were 'er poor circulation). Well, she woke-up, gabblin' words in a strange foreign lingo ('arriet thought it were Polish) and there was this fear in 'er eyes. She'd looked like a cornered animal. It took 'arriet an' me three more doses to get 'er out again. 'arriot were blinkin livid at the messiness of it all. I just felt a little sorry for the old bird an' even tried a smile, but that made 'er gabble even more. She struggled a bit but 'arriet held 'er down with a firm grip whilst I re-loaded the *'Exit Machine.'* Hmmm! I remember there was very little conversation that night – things were rather quiet between us. 'arriet just took 'erself off to the Olympic pool an' 'ad a marathon swimmin' session; she can't stand anythin' that's even a little disorderly. I'm glad 'arriet was on 'and to deal with the situation, she's so competent – Deidre would 'ave taken to pill-poppin' again.

Since then procedures 'ave been tightened-up so nothin' like that 'as 'appened again. Thankfully, we've 'ad an increase in relatives beggin' us to take on their *'terminal liabilities,'* so we get far less resistance from families than we used to. The worsening economic situation 'as increased the demand for our services. Families get by easier if they've no useless mouths to feed. With some o' the disposable minorities religion used to be a big factor, but who cares about God these days? Most o' those people with any religious views left at all 'ave either come round t' our way of thinkin' or 'ave vanished in a puff o' smoke! Poof! Religion gone! If memory serves me right we 'ad some sort of bearded big wig from Canterbury (I believe 'e was a retired Archbishop) come an' bless the first Dispatch Unit. Very ingratiating 'e were – but that were years ago when there were still the need to soothe 'n' calm the feelin's of relatives. There's no need for that now – that generation 'as gone – no one left 'oo cares enough to keep religion goin' in this part o' the world. Where they 'aven't been knocked down or converted into flats most churches are now *'Adult Pleasure Centres.'* Loads o' strange stuff goes on in 'em now – ahem! But that's another story.

'Are there still any political cases?'

Nah! None to speak of – as I said earlier, *The Old Jail'* does the 'igh rankin' political stuff. When the World Authorities decided to cut back on their Senior Civil Servants they went there – not t' the likes of us. 'eard from one o' the guards that they were more than a little aggrieved about bein' *'cut-back'* this way, convinced that the government were wantin' to save on redundancy payments. Yet, as mah contact said, they couldn't really complain 'cos they'd actually 'elped to put the 'ole system together in the first place! Strange that – bet they never dreamed that they'd be on the receivin' end o' things! Still – life 'as a funny way of turnin' out don't it? Unlike the *'common 'erd'* their families 'ad been allowed to claim their ashes for private internment for only a nominal fee. Apparently, this privilege was one o' the perks for 'avin' done the government certain favours in the past. I really 'oped it made their families feel better.

Also comin' down the pipeline were the economists. They'd displeased the World Authorities with their inaccurate forecasts of world growth. A spot check discovered that the *'the astrologer in residence'* was makin' more accurate predictions than they were so out they went! Mind yer, later it were the economists 'oo worked out exactly 'ow much would be saved through various trial dispatch programmes. Got things down to the last penny they did. They calculated the exact return to be made on each body part. 'owever once their usefulness was ended it was their turn to be economised!

'Have there been any protests against dispatching?'

When I first came here an outfit called *'The Human Defence League'* used to paint slogans on the walls of *The Old Jail'* – one in vivid pink read *'Old Jail – New Hell'* which I thought was in rather bad taste.

'ardly surprisingly the authorities didn't stand for that. Thanks to new techniques of *'Genetic Profile Surveillance,'* arrests were made and at a big *'show trial'* the accused were found guilty of *'displaying negative anti-social tendencies.'* After bein' made to clear off the graffiti with the gentle aid o' cattle prods they were given what we call *'a one way tour'* o' the Old Jail. I don't think that any of their families were able to reclaim their ashes. They'd not been good citizens yer see, no, no, not at all. This sort o' thing can't be seen to be rewarded. Nip it in the bud that's what I say.

'Do you encounter any criticism of your work?'

We still get a bit o' flack from the older generation. At a recent Wedding Reception for mah sister, 'er partner's father – a bit worse for drink, picked an argument wi' me and called me *'a minor functionary of death.'* I didn't mind the *'death'* bit but I found the word *'minor'* a little insultin'. Things could 'ave really blown up but for mah little sis's sake I bit mah lip an' just said *'Well, that's just your opinion.'* It was 'er third weddin' yer see an' she really wanted this relationship to work out. She'd asked me to be on mah best behaviour and t' stay off the booze. Still, I can't get over bein' called *'a <u>minor</u> functionary.'* 'oo does 'e think is? 'owever the likes of 'im will soon be gone.

'Do you work with the pre-teen group?'

Nah! We don't do children as a rule. They're usually consigned to *'The Old Jail'* where the political cases are kept. Between you an' me I hear it's a tough place to work. They used to 'ave long-servin' inmates do the job. (This was part o' some psychological experiment or other.) Apparently, things got out of 'and. There was, hmmm – how shall I say it, some *'tamperin' wi' the goods'* so the Unit was suspended and within days we received twelve 'dispatchees' from the jail, all covered wi' cuts an' bruises. Someone 'ad really knocked 'em about. But in my job it doesn't pay t' ask too many questions, it just pays to keep yer 'ead down an' obey whatever orders are given. I remember 'arriet divulging that they'd been given a very strong anaesthetic so they were *'out'* when we got 'em. She should know about that sort o' thing.

'What's the background of the pre-teen age group?'

Well, if dysfunctional families exceed their quota o' two children then their welfare payments are cut. If they can't sell the child for adoption (in most cases they can't) they come our way. A few go to the Joseph Life Care Institute in Stafford for *'research purposes.'* Some mothers don't like that because it 'as, shall we say, a bit of a *'reputation.'* But a small grant or a debt payment usually calms their conscience. Some mothers slip through the net an' make a livin' sellin' their children to *'The Joseph'* but they're the real unfeelin' sort. I don't mind dispatchin' pre-teen cargo if it 'as to be done but fiddlin' around with 'em for 'research purposes' is a bit much. *'The Joseph'* always takes care to dispose of its own unwanted *'specimens'* – we never get anythin' from 'em. They're a tightly closed shop. All I can say is that they seem to like takin' in twins and they 'ave a good name for organ transplants. Ageing zillionaires from across the world use the Institute's 'harvest' facilities so they can qualify for a *'Life Extension Permit.'* Some live to be a hundred and twenty but they pay dearly for this privilege an' sometimes things go wrong. One hair rejuvenator 'ad caused sheep's wool to spring up on this bloke's 'ead. There'd been a mix-up wi' the genetic samples. 'ooever did that must 'ave been a bit woolly-minded – hee-hee! I 'eard this from 'arriet 'oo told me that genetic crossing can still be a little unpredictable in its effects. One bloke even ended-up with the ears of a donkey, but personally I think that's a bit of a tall story. They do improve in the tellin' though, don't they?

'Are there any other issues needing to be considered?'

Well, at the present time there's somethin' of a t'do over containers an' the *'Crem.'* Typical of Accounts to get their 'oar in.' They're wantin,' in their wisdom, the present chipboard containers to be replaced by cardboard ones, on the grounds of environmental savings. Apparently, our local *'Crem'* stated that the new containers would reduce *'dissolution times'* by 3%. There's also talk o' tryin' this idea out in our Unit. *'Baldie Eagle'* is opposed; 'e says it would cause storage problems with the cargo. 'e actually sent a memo expressin' 'is misgivings ter *'the powers that be.'* 'owever, Management rarely listen t' the likes of us. The *'Crem'* is always gettin' on at us about somethin' or other and it's particularly bad when we place a major disposal order. They claim it interrupts their *'normal funeral arrangements'* (ones they can charge fat fees for). So it's become a bit of a standoff. I think it's this that's led t' the suggestion of more easily disposable containers. Personally, I can't see 'em workin' but 'oo am I to say? I'm only a little cog in a very big machine.

On a staff trainin' day we visited the *'Crem'* to 'ear about the new laser incineration process. Found 'em to be a dead serious lot, wi' *'dead'* bein' the operative word. Didn't even smile when I quipped *'Thar she blows!'* as one of our dispatches wafted out o' the chimney. I was told by mah supervisor that it weren't in good taste – but why not 'ave a laff t' lighten things up – that's wot I say? They also like to keep a lot o' the ashes themselves, for gardenin' purposes they say – but I 'ear a rumour that they sell 'em on t' private contractors for use as fertilizers. That seems a good idea as there's a growin' market for such goods in these days o' food shortages. As a perk we're sometimes allowed to keep a jar of ashes. I recycle them on mah old mum's rose bed though I never tell 'er where they come from. If she knew I think she'd faint straight out. She still 'as one or two old fashioned ideas – the elderly can't adapt the way we of the younger generation do. I'm already thinkin' o' arranging an 'ome dispatch for 'er. You can 'ave music an' that sort o' thing for those 'oo are goin' an' I wouldn't even 'ave to pay for the work that's done. It's one o' the best perks o' this job an' 'as just been made available – for *'unstinting devotion to duty'* they say.

'Have there been any problems in waste disposal?'

The real problem in disposal came when we dealt with the *'Ebola D'* wave. Apparently this bug 'ad mutated and no one knew 'ow to 'andle it. It were brought in by a migrant from the great famine in the Southern Regions. With these cases we 'ad to wear full protective gear an' we didn't 'alf look like bloomin' space walkers! (Even in these circumstances 'arriet an' I could 'ave a right laff!) We just about coped, but if there'd been more of 'em we'd 'a been sunk. 'owever, it still left us with a pile-up of unwanted cargo to contend with and more freezer trailers 'ad to be deployed. Accounts didn't like the extra expense an' Doctors objected to 'avin' their car spaces filled wi' these sorts o' vehicles – but what else could we do? It were an emergency an' anyone 'oo'd even remotely been in contact with the victims 'ad to be disposed of. We lost a lot of airport staff an' truck drivers that way. All this caused quite a stir – well yer can imagine the ruckus 'igh-up. Yet these migrants still keep comin' – they think our dispatch programmes create extra space 'an jobs for 'em. But thankfully, they 'elp keep the likes o' me an' Deidre busy. If business is slack, we always get sent a crop load of unwanted migrants t' dispose of.

'What do I think is most likely to change?'

Hmmm! There's the usual Management blather about cost savin's an' efficiency, but 'ow can we improve on those unless they automate everythin' to do with dispatchin'? Yet I feel that this line o' work requires 'the 'uman touch.' Doctors are to be allowed to administer 'ome dispatches if the family request it. Personally, I think this isn't nearly as efficient as our system but they 'ave to be given somethin' to do other than care for the curable cases. The only big jobs now are in Nano Medicine or in genetic re-assignment. Doctors could of course be put into a *'Dispatch Category'* but the government never knows when their services might be needed – I mean wot if another 'ealth scare comes along? It were the Doctors 'oo 'elped to contain the Ebola outbreak I just talked about. *'Virtual Medicare'* could take-up some o' the slack but not all of it. So Doctors are 'ere to stay although they grumble about 'avin' their status reduced to that of *'Waste Disposal Agents.'* In 'ealth, the old snobbery still lingers, an' us 'n' the medics don't see eye to eye. We always seem to remind 'em of just 'ow sidelined they've become. Yet funnily enough many of 'em were eager enough to promote despatchin' in the early days. They'd swallowed the government's promise o' new research facilities (with big grants to go with 'em) that were made at the time. Every man 'as 'is price and this were very true o' the Doctors. Give 'em a research grant an' they'll do almost anythin'.

'What have been the biggest changes?'

Oh, I don't know where to begin – the public are much more acceptin' of us these days, but beyond vastly improved efficiency I think the biggest change is in language. Wot I mean is – 'ow the 'ole death n' despatchin' thing 'as been described over the years. I remember 'ow *'death as a right'* became *'death as a recommendation'* and then *'death as a duty.'* Nowadays o' course, the word *'death'* 'as been dropped and we talk about *'constructive dispatch therapy'* which I think is far better, don't you? We can certainly cure all diseases! It's funny 'ow easily most people accept what, at one time 'ad been completely unacceptable; it's all part o' the adaptability of good old 'uman nature, I suppose.

'Are there any further comments?'

I love mah job; pay and conditions are good and I would recommend it t' anyone 'oo 'as, as Management says, a *'suitably positive outlook on life.'* I've been recommended for a Supervisor's post an' been told that mah dyslexia will no longer be viewed as 'n 'indrance. 'arriet always used to say that I 'ad potential but were always too *'laid back'* for mah own good. She used to scold me a little fer that. I'm certainly a good motivator an' mah workmates know me as *'the ever cheerful Kenny.'* (Ah like that!) I could still do with a little 'elp wi' the paperwork. Yes, I eagerly look forward to spendin' a good few years workin' for the Dignity Dispatch Service. It's a great career if, of course, yer know which 'buttons' to press!

Interlude: We Shall Live

We shall live in a mass extermination society
Where death as a right will become death as a duty

The old, infirm and terminally ill
All targets for a mass-medical kill

Those deemed a *'burden to the State'*
Will find euthanasia to be their fate

The unwanted elderly with money in the bank
Now due to die with grasping relatives to thank

Patients tremble with helpless dread
Soon they'll be among the discarded dead

White coated staff prepares a lethal injection
Their humanity now in a state of subjection

Mini-Shipman's they've all become
With heavy sedation their victims are numb

Another useless life to finish
The unwanted definitely will diminish

Drug administration, all done by machine
Psychologically, that's much more clean

Termination targets to complete
Now the disabled begin to deplete

White coat brutality is the norm
No longer any conscience to be borne

Teams compete to terminate quicker
Ensuring that life won't continue to flicker

Bored administrators complete the paperwork
Important duties they dare not shirk

No Nuremburg trial they're having to face
With names as statistics on a secret data base

As hospital mortuaries fill up
Financial budgets must add up

Funds allocated to buy a new freezer lorry
Pungent smells had caused some worry

Spare body parts can be extracted
Helpful laws have been enacted

No worries about a compensation claim
There's no one around to take the blame

In this country compassion has fled
The *'mildly sick'* may soon join the dead

A fresh government decree adds names to a list
Including political dissenters – they do insist

Cardboard coffins will now be mandatory
Highly ecological and highly inflammatory

They will increase any saving
Resulting in fewer bills needing paying

It's our evolutionary duty to eliminate the weak
Our species won't be propagated by the meek

Good and evil each comprise the 'Cosmic One'
And into its blissful 'Nirvana' we shall all come

Auschwitz-Birkenau provided a terrible warning
But why should we bother with endless mourning

Just forget the million plus who were slain
Thinking about them causes too much pain

Once death was inflicted by stealth
Now it's free on the National Health

Dignitas' laid the groundwork
Painful duties it did not shirk

The media was full of helpful fools
For our cause they provided useful tools

Celebrity endorsement was the key
They generously waivered any fee

Do it yourself' death was boldly sold
All human love was growing cold

The unwanted dead go up in billowing smoke
Give crematoria furnaces a good old stoke!

Perhaps some use for them can be found
Otherwise let's scatter the ashes on the ground

Compassion has died, politicians have lied
Nowhere to hide from the euthanasia tide

The future ain't gonna be much fun
'Cos' in the end, we'll all 'get done'

We're becoming a mass extermination society
Where death as a right is now death as a duty

We're becoming a mass extermination society

La-la-la

CHAPTER 2: THE DIGNITY SUITE

The scene begins with a shot of a heavily tanned Kenny. He's relaxed and smiling as he strolls through a crowded airport terminal, trundling a suitcase behind him with an oversized teddy bear tucked under his right arm. He's sporting a rather ridiculous straw hat and a short-sleeved floral shirt with cream knee-length shorts. It's evident he's returning from what looks to have been a holiday in hot climes. The background clamour is full of the noise of loud-speaker announcements and of aircraft preparing to take off or land. He looks plumper than when we last met him, but there's still that self-satisfied, warm and disarming smile on his face. The scene then switches to the room with the microphone on the table. There are now four empty coffee cups on the chest of drawers and a crumpled chocolate wrapper adorning the pale green plate. The large teddy bear is now sitting upright at the bottom of the bed. Once again Kenny presses a few keys and lightly taps the head of the microphone. The female voice begins its staccato questions and commands: - "Please give your full name."

'ello again! 'as it been over a year since we last spoke? Well fancy that! I've gone-up in the world since then an' become a Unit Supervisor! Great-eh?

'You're wonderin' about this sun tan?' Well – I've just come back from a fortnight's 'oliday in Euro Province, South West Isle Two (it used to be called Majorca). 'ad a great time on the beach an' 'pullin.' I got someone very special a big teddy bear but shhh! I won't say 'oo. I felt a real 'narna' carryin' it through the airport in front o' global surveillance an' all o' those fancy security cameras. But I know you're gonna want t' ask me about mah work, so as we say in the business, *Let's press the buttons an' get goin!'*

'How's it been over the last year?'

Up and down really. There's all this talk of a *'new wave'* as the government's capped the right of life at 73 and a quarter unless you're in a high income group an' can buy exemption. This gives yer a final two years t' enjoy yer retirement an' get things in order before

– hey presto – you're gone! They call this latest measure *'lifetime rationalisation.'* So we're gonna to be gettin' a wave o' the recently retired. It's already seen mah old mum out too, I were allowed t' arrange a cosy 'ome dispatch for 'er free o' charge. She wanted 'er last view to be o' the roses which she could see from 'er bedroom window – she always loved 'er little rose garden. (Ah spread her ashes on 'em.) Was most touched by *'The Happy Exit Day'* card I got from mah colleagues. (It 'ad 'er face on a balloon floatin' up to the sky – I've still got it.) Regardin' the future, there could be a switch to more young offenders or the children o' 'dysfunctional' families. (By the way *'dysfuntional'* seems to mean whatever the government wants it to mean.) Oh, and their parents too. But 'oo knows? We'll just 'ave t' wait an' see.

'What have been the ups?'

Well I got promoted to Supervisor but I'll tell you more about that later. At long last we've 'ad our walls painted a pastoral pink as it were judged to be more psychologically soothing fer the staff. They've even laid in piped music, 'andel, Mozart an' all that crew. I were amazed at wot a bit o' music could do! It makes the 'ole place far more relaxin' – very considerate o' Management I'd say. Don't 'ave to *jolly things* along so much now. 'owever, I hear Management want to knock down the adjoining walls so as they can double capacity. That's typical – they no sooner do somethin' up, than they want to knock it down again. Rumour 'as it that countries of the Eastern Regions want to send some o' their unwanted surplus our way – 'ow they'd do this I just dunno. Must all be to do wi' global politics, but all that's way above my 'ead. I don't bother t' think about such matters. Why should I? A'm 'appy in mah job!

'Have there been any other ups?'

Well, we look set t' beat that other Unit from across the road. They've been caught 'andlin' their figures a bit too creatively shall we say. They 'ad an agreement with the porters to wheel in some *'natural dispatches'* to their room so they could be placed onto their databases;

'uppin'' their figures, so to speak. They got a little too ambitious for their own good don't you think? But thanks to *'The Regional Accounts Department'* discrepancies were found and now they're bein' threatened wi' *'trolleyfication.'* It's cleared the way fer us t' go for the Regional Target Prize and I think this explains the latest investments. The Finance Department, under its new chief, Mr Lehman Bean, aven't been exactly pleased because they're always tryin' t' find new ways to save money. Well, they can't ave it both ways can they? If a thing's worth investin' in then yer back it all the way. That's simple, aint it?

Personally speakin' the biggest *'up'* 'as been mah own promotion – now that really put a rosy tint on everythin'. I got it after just one interview – not the usual two or three before you're considered. Well, if I'm really honest, I've got to admit I were walkin' into dead men's shoes.

'How did I get the Supervisor's job?'

Well, as I say, it all went surprisin'ly easy. I got it just after mah last 'oliday and it took just one interview. Apparently, after I'd gone on leave (an' thankfully, all unbeknown to me, blissfully sunning mahself on the beach) all 'ell 'ad let loose back at work – forgive the French. To quote the old sayin' *'trouble comes in threes'* an' it certainly did fer us! Luckily as I say, I were well out of it. You remember me sayin' that those environmentally friendly cardboard containers would cause problems? Well they did! Apparently one of our migrant porters failed to notice that a leg were pokin' out from the bottom o' one of 'em. The cargo 'ad been wrongly recorded as a double amputee case when in fact 'e were a single one. The result was that (for economical reasons) 'e'd been placed into too small a container – trunk size so to speak, with no *'leg room'* – again forgive the pun. So there 'e was, this porter, wheelin' this item t' one of the freezer vans with this blackened leg covered with boils pokin' out for all t' see. As you can well imagine it didn't exactly gladden the 'earts o' those few relatives visitin' their loved ones. Yer can jest imagine their faces as that trolley went by. The porter's excuse was that, as only one leg were showin' 'e didn't think much upset would be caused by it. The porter also made a point o' sayin' that 'e kept a good eye on the leg, makin' sure it didn't knock into anythin' or anybody. Well 'e certainly put *'is foot in it!'* 'ardly surprisingly, Management went ballistic an' so 'e was 'despatched to a more permanent position' (as we say o' failed employees). I could 'ave told 'em that the policy of 'avin *'educationally challenged'* migrants, barely able to speak the President's English just wouldn't work. Mah former Supervisor, *'Baldie Eagle'* used to express strong views on the subject. Kept nattering onto Management but all they ever did were t' natter back to 'im about 'budgetary reasons.'

We could 'ave ridden out that storm by blamin' the porters, which we did – but the very next day, would you *'Adam' an' 'Eve'* it an even bigger load o' bother 'appened! Senior Management were conductin' a tour wi' this little geezer from Switzerland 'oo were advising us on efficiency improvements. Well, as 'e walked past to visit our room a 24 stone male item popped out of 'is container an' landed straight onto 'im, knockin' im clean over! Apparently 'e swore loudly in German, as our Managers – all embarrassed like – were liftin' 'im up. Even worse, the item 'ad been a multiple 'ernia case an' some of its contents 'ad poured out, spoilin' this man's expensive black suit! Not 'elpin' matters were Deidre 'oo just fainted clean away when she popped out t' see what were goin' on! You could see it as a bit of a laff really; there was this little Swiss geezer swearin' in German as 'e struggled under this item whose contents were runnin' all over 'is suit; then there was Senior Management lookin' deathly pale in shock and then Deidre stood in front of 'em, 'avin' an 'ysterical swoon. A right comedy it must 'a been – so long as it weren't you o'course! I even 'eard that this little Swiss bloke 'ad stood there, all glowerin' as Senior Management 'ad tried 'ard to brush the goo off 'is fancy pin-striped suit. 'is gold rimmed spectacles 'ad been bent as well. From the glare in 'is eyes it were obvious that he'd 'ave liked to 'ave dispatched the 'ole lot of 'em! Funny lot the Swiss, they 'elp to start up all this dispatchin' business in the first place, but they sure 'as 'eck don't like it when it all goes *'belly-up'* so ter speak!!

Yer can just imagine the blame game that were on. We blamed the porters for placin' the cargo in an unstable vertical, rather than the authorized 'orizontal position. The porters denied all knowledge o' this and then we tried t' blame *'Accounts'* for demandin' the use o' these *'Ecologicaly Friendly'* containers. Sadly, *'Accounts'* are too useful to the organization to be dispensed with.

That business did for Deidre. Next mornin' she were found dead in the rubbish area. Apparently, she'd got onto the 'ospital roof an' jumped off. 'ow she got up there no one knows. Perhaps it were security bein' careless again. They say there were a note in 'er pocket about not bein' able to take anymore. Would surprise me if there really was a note 'cos she could 'ardly string two words together – would always give one word answers 'n never want to look at yer. I don't mind 'er toppin' 'erself if she were that way inclined, but did she 'ave to embarrass the Unit? Never could figure 'er out. The enquiry into 'er death came to no conclusion as to 'er motive. They never do. Mind you, if I'd been around I'd 'ave tried t' talk 'er out of it. Or if she'd still felt so inclined I would 'ave put in a good word an' arranged an easier dispatch. At least that way we could 'ave sent 'er relatives a nice *'Happy Exit Day'* card. I think she were makin' some sort o' statement, but that's the trouble wi' women – they never can think things through calmly like us blokes do.

Yer can imagine that there were somethin' of an atmosphere when I got back from Majorca (sorry, Euro Province, South West Isle Two – the old names stick better with me). Activities 'ad been suspended until an *'Operational Review'* 'ad been completed and mah predecessor *Baldie Eagle* didn't look too 'appy neither. Two days after I got back 'e called to *The Old Jail* for a disciplinary hearin' an' we were told that *'e'd been 'transferred to a post more suited for 'is capabilities.'* I thought this was a bit unfair as 'e'd been a good boss, recommending me for promotion an' such like. Oddly enough, I never did see anythin' of 'im again. Thought I caught sight of 'is fancy fur lined coat bein' sold in the 'ospital charity shop on the 'igh street but I could be wrong as 'is collection of false fur lined coats is somethin' 'e'd never willin'ly give up. Also saw what looked like 'is 'ome made trycycle bein' auctioned on the 'Now-Buy' cloud site. Obviously floggin' it t' get money – so 'e must 'ave bin fired – but in our occupation that term can mean more than one thing. It's always the custom with Management to blame someone less senior. I certainly couldn't imagine Dr Galton bein' exactly forgivin' when 'e 'ad t' issue a fulsome apology and pay fer that Swiss guy's suit an' glasses. 'e were probably worried about 'is peerage if things got out t' the media – but fortunately for 'im, influential friends ensured that they didn't. 'e's a man of many connections our Galton is.

Anyway, I got a few days extra 'ome leave as they decided the fate o' the Unit. Then 'oo should call me out o' the blue but 'arriet – yes the Harriet!!! 'adn't 'eard from 'er for over three years an' 'er first words were *'Hello Kenny, my dah-ling mentor, do you remember me?'* 'ow could I forget that posh totty voice of 'ers? She's now taken-up 'orse ridin'. Anyway, after we spent some time catchin' up on some old news she invited me for interview for the newly vacant Supervisor's post. (She's now someone big in 'uman Resources.) She felt that someone with my *'positive attitude'* would be *'an indispensible help'* in *'tidying-up this ghastly mess'* an' gettin' dispatches goin' again. It a good sign that the interview weren't in *'The Old Jail'* – that would 'ave put the wind up me if it were! Anyway, I were called before this panel of three, one of 'em was a work psychologist from the Milgram Institure 'oo looked vaguely lost (they often do), the other (the scowling guy in the centre) was a deputy of Dr Galton's and next to 'im was Lehman Bean ('oo kept nattering on about savin's). Oh, an' 'arriet there too – and she gave me a very welcomin' smile. She's certainly gone far, an' fer the first time she wore make-up and smelt o' this expensive perfume. I think she were tryin' t' impress me. She's a real lady! Well, she went t' great lengths t' point out mah positive qualities and 'usefulness' t' the other members o' the panel. She even winked at me a couple o' times in 'er flirtatious way. That lady certainly 'as class! After that the interview were a formality and I got the job an' a 10% pay rise. 'Great!' I thought – that were the best job interview I ever 'ad in mah life! I punched the air when I knew I'd got it! Lehman didn't look too 'appy but 'e never does; 'es a typical accountant. Rumour 'as it 'e wants to 'rationalize' our little Unit out of existence. So that's it all sorted out. Baldie Eagle gone and me in 'is place. Funny 'ow nicely things turn out, eh?

'How did you find the Supervisors' Training Course?'

Oh that, yeh, it were pretty good I suppose. We 'ad a Residential Trainin' in some remote castle in Euro Province, Anglo South West Two (it used to be called *'Devon'*). We actually 'andled those old fashioned things called 'books,' (not seen one for years.) Maybe some o' the 'istory of our work is judged to be *'too sensitive'* to go into electronic form. There'd also bin lawyers arguments about such things as copyright and data protection. When those lawyers get into things they always slow 'em down. We should dispatch more of 'em – I would dance a jig every time I pressed a button, 'specially if it were a divorce lawyer. (The one the *'ex'* got nearly ruined me.)

'Did you find anything of particular interest?'

Well, what really interested me about this Course were the 'istory session we 'ad about our work. I din't know 'ow much we owed to pioneer movements like *'Dignitas,'* *'Exit'* and *'The Euthanasia Association.'* It were really interestin' 'ow, by gradual, *'little by little'* steps, they created *'a climate of opinion'* in which our sort o' work first became tolerated, then fully accepted and finally *'mandatory.'* (Although the British Medical Association 'ad to be bought off with a generous pay settlement for Doctors and promises o' grants for 'enhanced organ therapy.') It were all done ever so subtily. The marketin' for what was then called *'Assisted Suicide'* and *'Euthanasia'* was flamin' brilliant! Usin' terminally ill celebrities an' well-loved actors as advocates all 'elped in gettin' our cause accepted. I remember 'avin' seen' one particular celebrity on a pro-euthanasia video they once showed to our class at school. I can't remember 'is name now but it 'elped pave the way for ma present career. (Seein' the first real life assisted suicide on the good ol' BBC made it all look so natural.) They really knew 'ow to pull on the 'eart strings. (Of course nothin' was said about the need to make savin's or reduce budgetary costs – that would 'ave bin unacceptable back then.) It were all these pressure groups like *'Dignitas'* and former TV companies like *'The BBC'* 'oo 'elped create the world we live in today. It's amazin' 'ow a little killin' quickly becomes acceptable. I know it sounds daft now but back then they didn't seem to ask the obvious question *'who should do the killin'?'* It were just a case o' gently coaxin' the *'dispatchee'* into takin' the lethal dose fer themselves – I mean that's really inefficient by our standards. Still, the point that anyone sufferin' from a *'general weariness of life'* could freely apply for an assisted suicide provided a very useful precedent for those wishin' to expand the service. The term could be used to cover just about everyone not blest with my cheery outlook on matters. At first, the medical profession were reluctant t' get themselves involved. Their argument were that it would change the nature o' their profession – weren't it supposed t' be more concerned wi' the <u>preservation</u> rather than the <u>takin'</u> of life? The Doctors got all 'igh an' mighty about that! Family carers were often too distressed to do the job or if they'd end up makin' a botched mess o' things an' this risked causin' ill feelin' within the deceased's family. In the end, the only realistic answer were to create a special body o' people 'oo were psychologically suited fer the task. Obviously, they 'ad to 'ave the right personal disposition but at least they'd get on wi'the job in an efficient way it would also allow for most o' the medical profession to keep their distance an' t' maintain the trust o' their curable patients. I also think the solution of recruitin' people from the fringes of that profession was rather clever. They 'ad the expertise but also managed to keep their distance. One bloke I felt really sorry for were that Doctor 'arold Shipman geezer – turned out 'e were years ahead of 'is time – although 'is activities were tiny by today's standards. Galton is pressin' for a statue of 'im to be erected on the site of 'is old surgery but there's some local opposition. Certain narrow-minded people took the 'uff when told it would 'old a syringe squirtin' pink coloured water every hour. (The idea was to attract tourists.) I think o' 'im as a role model all medical staff could do wi' followin'. In mah 'onest opinion, that Shipman were a much misunderstood man. Today, e'd be one of our Directors. I must say it's funny 'ow things can change so much, an' so quickly too!

'Was there anything you didn't like about the course?'

Eh, well I didn't exactly take t' the theory an' neither did the other Trainee Supervisors. This side o' things were given by a certain Doctor Eagle-Hare Lapwing from the Zimbardo Memorial Faculty in Stanford University, California. (Apparently 'e adopted this name to symbolise 'is belief in what 'e called *'the Transcendental Oneness of Nature.'*) 'e wore this red poncho thing, green tights, a necklace made o' sea shells and earrings in the shape o' Dolphins! I mean, worra a laff – we were near t' bursting! Oh, an' e' also wore this black an' white striped wig thing with a pigtail which kept slidin' down the side of 'is 'ead. Yer wouldn't be surprised t' hear that 'e was a motivational psychologist with a Post Doctorate in Dispatch Studies. 'e'd also done work for the Milgram Memorial Institute. From what I could make out, 'is argument that our work just as *'life affirming'* ('e kept usin' that expression) as the work of a midwife. Whereas a midwife 'elped to *'birth'* people inter this world, we 'elp to *'birth'* (that were another word 'e kept usin') 'em into a *'higher realm of reality.'* 'e said they would be *'one'* with the *'Cosmic Consciousness'* that sustains *'the Trans-dimensional Multiverse.'* We would be 'elpin' to promote both the *'physical and spiritual evolution'* of 'umanity. At the very least we would be releasin' souls for the next stage o' their re-incarnation cycle, whatever that meant. 'e also kept 'arpin' on about 'ow, what's known as *'The Human Sustainability Industry'* should be re-named *'The Life Affirming Industry.'* 'e were quite 'eated on that point. *'Spoke with passion'* as someone remarked.

I think 'is idea is that, through a process of *'relentless culling'* ('e loved that term) we'll all at last attain an *'ascended'* or *'deified'* humanity. In other words, by *'knocking off'* the unwanted, those remainin' will evolve into *'ascended beings'* and then *'little gods,'* floatin' around what 'e called *'the Omega Cosmos.'* (Don't ask me what it means, I' 'aven't a clue.) I mean 'ow can they be *'ascended beings'* if they're still alive? Anyway, all this 'ogwash reminds me o' the daft notions the evil villains 'ad in those old Sci-fi movies; where they were always wantin' t' take over everythin' – t' rule the 'ole world and that sort of thing! The trouble with too much education is that it can take away yer

down to earth, good old fashioned common sense. To me it's simple
– *'we cull in order t' survive.'*

T' the others as well all this mumbo-jumbo were a bit borin' – there's
no need to justify our work like this. In my 'umble opinion the 'ole
thing boils down to a matter o' savin' money an' increasin'
sustainability in order t' preserve the 'uman race. *'Evolutionary wheels of
life'* an' what 'ave you, just don't come into it for me. Overall, I would
say that this session was memorable more for the teacher than for 'is
teachin'. Me and some o' the other lads passed notes with bets round,
wonderin' whether what 'e called *'is 'beaver wig'* would fall off. 'arriet –
yeah, she were there too – didn't I mention? Well, surprises all round,
she really took to 'im! I 'eard 'er gushin' to this Eagle-Hare Lapwing
about *'how amazingly profound'* 'is perspective was when 'e talked about
'higher plains of life.' She praised 'im for displayin' *'such wonderfully clear
and positive thinking.'* She was like a simperin' school girl! In response 'e
actually gave what I thought could be a smile (at least 'is lips curled
upwards). Mind you our 'arriet 'as always liked the intellectual side o'
things. It comes wi' bein' a Doctor, I suppose. Mahself? I prefer the
more down t' earth approach.

'How were the other sessions?'

Thankfully they were better than Lapwing's. There was a really
interestin' talk given by this geeky bloke from the Macro-Gates
Foundation at Oregon, Now what were 'e called? Ah, Bill Bright –
yeh that's it. 'e were an expert in Dispatch Engineering, an 'e pointed
out all the technical developments that lay in the 'not too distant'
future. Couldn't make out all 'e said but most of it really interestin'.
What appears to be in the offin' is *'Nano Multiple Cargo Disposal'*
(Yeah, I know it's a mouthful). It's a bran' new type of Exit Machine.
It's got a small tube attached to a micro-security camera. Well – it
shoots a 'Nano Exit Bug' (or NEB) through this tiny tube. In
millionths of a second it's in the Service User's bloodstream without
any need for an injection. The client's gone before you can count up
to three. Then we're left with a choice – we can use the technology to
consume everythin' within a few seconds ('specially useful in

infectious diseases cases) an' send the remainin' gunge t' the toxic waste dumps in the Southern Regions or we can shoot in some other Nano bugs to convert the cargo into a glutinous jelly which can then be siphoned away to a plant that can re-cycle it into ecologically friendly fertilizer. Everythin will 'appen in a soundproof and darkened room so we needn't see or hear a thing. We'd 'ave complete separation from the Cargo. Psychologically, this was *judged to be conducive to staff morale.'* This technology would also 'elp in crowd control. If you 'ave a drunken crowd causin' aggravation in a town centre you just fire in a few NEB's an' the problem's dealt with. The police representative certainly liked the idea. In 'is own words, *"It would facilitate 'Crowd Calming' by reducing the number of 'disruptive elements.'"* Personally, I think they should try it out on the English Football Team 'oo came last in the World Cup Qualifiers again – beaten five nil by San Marino. What a disgrace! I thought bein' beaten three nil by Andorra were bad enough!

Eventually robotic Dispatch Units will come in. We all know it's just around the corner. It became clear as crystal that our own role would 'ave to change. Our expertise would 'ave to switch to *'Community Dispatching.'* This method is just another form of Dispatchin' for those 'oo can afford it in the comfort of their own 'ome or in some place that makes 'em feel more at ease. If it's wanted there's even some nice music provided to create an atmosphere of peace – just as 'appened with dear old mum. Obviously, these services require a fee and there's an extra (optional) fee for *'individualised service user removal.'* The term used for all of this was *'Bespoke Dispatching;'* all tailored to the needs of the 'soon to be dispatched.' It's always the same – new technology means job losses. We were reassured by bein' told that the lower grades were the only target. Supervisors' positions seemed secure enough although we'd be required to be 'adaptable.' Personally, I like the idea of bein' a *'Community Dispatch Officer.'* It would get me out 'n' about. I particularly enjoyed the promotional video, featuring the new technology. It was backed-up by some very stirrin' music which 'arriet told me was 'The William Tell Overture.' She said it was by some guy called Rossini 'oo I think was some big pop star in the 1960s, although I must say I'd never 'eard of 'im. '60's classical music is enjoyin' somethin' of a revival at present.

'What will electronic dispatching involve?'

Now that we've made all these breakthroughs with the 'uman mind – yer know – thinkin' an' all that – there's plans t'use *'Nano-Suggestion Implants.'* They look set to be right clever little beasties – I mean, would you *'Adam an' Eve it'* when they're activated they actually persuade those down for cullin' to 'willingly' participate in their own demise! Strange or wot! If these plans go ahead what'll 'appen is this – the implants 'll give 'em an overwhelming urge to attend what's goin' t' be called a *'Drop In Release Centre.'* Once there they'll be all too pleased to walk between two large conveyer belts. Then – with no fuss – they'll quietly strip down to their underwear and place their belongin's into a box (conveniently positioned on one of the conveyor belts, ready for removal). After that they'll *'freely'* lie down on the other conveyor belt. Once they're lyin' there all quiet-like an operative in the office overlookin' the plant will 'switch on' the *'one way'* sleep programme embedded in the 'Nano Implants.' These'll provide the 'service users' with 'appy dreams as they drift off into a deep sleep, then a coma, and then it's all done. (It takes another three minutes t' ensure all brain activity 'as ceased.) Soon a buzzer 'll sound and they'll be carted-off to a laser or an acid-based disposal facility. (There's the usual debate about which is the most efficient.) Their belongin's are then recycled or sold back to relatives for payment of a fee. It's estimated that each 'run' could dispose of up to 2,000 *'service-users'* within twenty t' thirty minutes! Yeah, honest – would yer just credit it? Some of the 'service user conveyors' are really long and 'ave lots of smaller, circular conveyors for the luggage so a huge amount of cargo can be despatched all at once. Soft music 'll be playin' all the while t' give a relaxed atmosphere an' make it feel less like a factory run. Every little bit 'elps don't it?

One other thing – the 'powers that be' are backin' these nifty implants 'cos it'll mean they don't 'ave t' go t' the expense of employin' armed guards. The *'service users'* <u>voluntarily</u> hand themselves over for disposal so they'll no 'argy-bargy' fightin' against the inevitable! The little implants should make sure they feel perfectly blissful about exitin' this life! All very clever, if I may say so. I like the efficiency of the idea, but where that leaves more 'traditional dispatchers' like *'yours truly,'* is open to debate. I was glad when, after the presentation, 'arriot turned round t' me 'n' said, *'Don't worry my dear there'll always be a need for someone with your splendid record.'* That was funny – she's never called me *'my dear'* before nor spoken to me in such a warm manner. I couldn't 'elp wonderin' whether I caught a look o' pity in 'er eyes. She seemed to go out of 'er way to make sure that I was 'avin' an 'appy time, which I was in a way.

'What is the purpose of electronic dispatching?'

We were told that the 'ole idea was to *'integrate the dispatch process'* – to make it super-efficient an' ultra-'ygienic. ('arriet 'specially liked the last point; I could see 'er smilin' an' gettin' all excited. She always did <u>hate</u> untidiness.) There'll be 'ardly any need for porters or for the *'Crem.'* (They won't like that.) Despite some 'assle in determinin' the exact physical meltdown rates, the real problem seemed to centre around security. In what used to be America, a disgruntled operative 'ad stolen some Dispatch Bugs and posted 'em to Bankers. So all these bankers 'ad suddenly started turnin' into jelly (or more usually it was their unpaid interns) in all their fancy offices an' the Stock Exchange began to plummet. Things got really bad when the World Governing Authorities were targeted and its new 'eadquarters in Jerusalem 'ad to close for a month. By the time the Security Services 'ad tracked this man down it were too late. When they stormed 'is 'ome in Washington they just found a load o' jelly in the bath. E'd done 'imself in which was perhaps wise given the treatment 'e would 'ave 'ad from their Alaskan Bay Detention Centre. (They never did get to know 'ow 'e'd got 'old o' the NEB's; but e'd been able to replicate 'em with the aid of a Terminator Games Programme 'e'd made.) All this was kept quiet at the time an' the incident was conveniently blamed on those foreign terrorists 'oo later 'took out' part o' Washington DC (the capital of the former USA). 'owever, this attack did delay the introduction of this new technology for some years until certain security issues were resolved. Fortunately, this is now the case 'n' a trial robotic plant 'as been established in Death Valley. Animal experiments were a success and now they're tryin' things out on unwanted migrants from what used to be called Mexico. Early results are promisin'. Europe's to open its own *'Continental Site'* – where the old 'adron Collider used to be. It's deep underground and that's thought to offer a greater security advantage. We even 'ave a small pilot plant in West Celtic Island One (formerly Anglesey) – 'arriet gleefully told me that it was the place where Ancient Druids used to perform their ritual 'uman sacrifices – ugh! Nowadays, we've a far more advanced way of doin' things. Transport 'owever appears to be an issue – although surplus cargo could always be deposited in the Celtic Sea to encourage fish breeding. Overall, I think this pilot sheme looks very promisin'.

I thought that Bill Bright's session was great. Like mah late dad I'm interested in electrical things, at one time I actually thought about becomin' an electrician, but no work was ever available. Migrant workers 'ad got all the jobs. Mind you 'arriet looked a bit down in the mouth. I think it was because she could see the distinctive 'ands on approach to 'er work, (which she enjoys) just slippin' away from her. She also complained that all this made our approach in the former United Kingdom *'appear rather amateurish.'* I chipped in there, sayin' that we do our best but 'ad to admit that we've some way to go before becomin' really world class in what's gonna to be rebranded as *The Human Sustainability Industry.'* (When I first started it was called the *'Mercy Care Industry.'*) 'oo nars whether fundin' is available for all o' this, but it usually appears like magic when the New World Authorities want to consign some segment of 'umanity to the *'Unwanted Waste'* category. They can be quite generous at such times.

'Were there any other developments on the Residential Course?'

One big piece o' news announced at the Conference were that Galton's got 'is peerage; 'e's now *'Lord Galton of Down.'* We all gave 'im a big round of applause which 'e seemed to appreciate but 'e still 'ad 'is grim death mask expression on. Perhaps 'e guessed 'e's only got five years at the most t' enjoy 'is seat in The Lords. (This is the maximum term allowed to peers before they're forced to enjoy a more permanent retirement.) 'e also 'as to work a six month notice before it takes effect, cos 'e needs to take time groomin' a successor. That development 'as left a question mark 'angin' over everyone's future; 'avin' a new chief can be very unsettlin' – in my book it usually means a raft o' redundancies.

'What happened after the Residential Course?'

When I got back from the Conference to take up the new post I found that the old Dignity Room 'ad been re-named *'The Dignity Suite.'* It' ad been substantially refurbished in the way I've already described. All this were done at 'arriet's 'instigation 'oo now views our room as bein' *'a womb in which to birth people into a higher plain of divine consciousness,'* whatever that means. (Been listenin' to too much guff from Lapwing, I suspect.) She also felt we could do with a more *'user friendly image.'* Since I began as Supervisor she drops in every other Friday afternoon *'to have a go on the buttons'* as she calls it. She always looks 'appier after this an' says *'it sets me up for a jolly weekend of horse riding.'* Sometimes we talk about the old times – *'the pre-Deidre days'* as I call 'em. The odd time she's back to bein' the gigglin' 'arriot I once knew, 'specially when she drops those stiff 'uman Resource Director manners an' starts chattin' about 'er work. She keeps sayin' *'how amusing'* and *'entertaining'* I am. Like me, the DDS is the centre of 'er life, treatin' it like family. Marriage for her will be a career move. She'll swan off with some 'igh rankin' Director or other. Even with the recent promotion, she's still way above the likes o' me. Didn't think I'd ever feel soft with a woman after the *'ex'* but desire can take many forms. Although 'arriet move on to 'igher things I'm sure she'll 'ave me one o' these fine days.

'Other developments since I became Supervisor?'

Well, the first priority was to find a replacement for poor distracted Deidre. Even with 'arriet in charge 'uman Resources 'ad to scrape the bottom o' the barrel an' so we got lumbered with Sharon. She's the one person 'oo actually provokes me to wan' Deidre back! I can see why we're goin' to need robots, although Sharon is bit of a robot – in manners I mean. She's fifty-somethin', overweight an' 'as a face resembling a slab o' concrete. With 'er it's either all sullen silences or complaints about 'ow the work affects 'er nerves or 'er legs. She once lifted 'er skirt 'n' showed me all 'er varicose veins. After that I asked 'er to come to work in trousers. She also 'as an annoyin' 'abit of chompin' on 'er false teeth – said she couldn't afford denture implants. (Personally, I think 'arriet got in an operative 'oo she knew I wouldn't strike up a personal relationship with. She knows mah taste in these things.) As Supervisor I'd access to Sharon's file an' found out that she was the lady involved in some child kidnap scandal years back. After that she were given the usual option o' bein' one of our *'Service Consumers'* or workin' for us under an assumed name – naturally she chose the latter; so that's 'ow she came to us – worst luck! Oddly enough, since she came we started to get some pre-teen cases. That's usually *'The Old Jail's'* work but it's currently bein' refurbished with some new technology or other so some of its cargo's been shifted onto us. Weren't too keen at first but a job's a job so I've no option but t' get on with it. 'owever, I usually leave this business to Sharon 'oo tends to perk up a little when given 'em. She gives a rather sly smile when they breathe their last. Now, now ... I wonder whether she was the lady behind *'the babes in the garden case'* I 'ead about years back? It caused a sensation then; the media were full of it; they found six of 'em. Hmm! It could be 'er (although if it is, she's aged a lot) an' they don't always tell you everythin' in the *'confidential files.'*

'Are there any staff problems?'

Although Sharon gets on wi' the job, I can't delegate any o' the admin' tasks to 'er, as I could wi' Deidre ('oo were always good in that line). Sharon's a bit slow you see. I contacted 'arriet about the problem an' as usual she was very understandin'. She mentioned she was promotin' a new scheme in which *'The Dignity Suite'* would be integrated into Medical Trainin'. This means that all those applyin' for a License to practice Medicine or Senior Nursin' will be required to do a three month placement in a DDU. 'er idea is t' ensure that our work becomes completely acceptable wi' the younger generation o' Medics. Any *unhelpful 'them an' us' barrier would be completely removed;* for me the benefit would be a higher calibre of operatives. All I 'ad to do was to 'old on until the new arrangements ground their way through the system. The Auxiliary Sub-committee's response 'ad been 'ighly favourable and it's already on Galton's desk, 'with 'im recommendin' it to 'is successor. She giggled when she warned that she certainly wouldn't be sendin' any attractive female Medics my way. One was enough for mah needs! 'er response brightened the 'ole day f' me – that's what I like about 'arriet – she gets things done. I think 'er idea will be very successful because, with the prisons virtually empty and mostly due for closure, we're runnin' out o' the Deidres and Sharons o' this world. Their day's over.

'How did you attempt to deal with these problems?'

Well, to cheer Sharon up I got permission to take a picture of 'er standing beside a trolley with one of our service users on it. She'd been goin fer ages about wantin' a souvenir of 'er work. Told me it was for 'er family, (as if she 'ad any). She even 'ad 'opes it would might be used for a recruitment poster. I wish I'd never bothered! It was lucky everythin was quiet! She spent hours slapping on make-up tryin' to make 'er face look presentable and choosing the uniform she thought would suit 'er best. She dyed 'er hair a flamin' bright ginger for the occasion! Getting 'er to smile in such a way that 'er false teeth didn't drop out was a problem. Not only that! I 'ad to fiddle around with the image to get' to make her look even semi-presentable but after some touching up it didn't come out at all bad. (I've always been good at that sort of thing.) It showed 'er the way she wanted to be shown. She was more or less 'appy for an hour or two after that. Come to think of it the woman in *'the babes in the garden case'* had been found out because she kept certain *'mementos.'* I think some of 'em included photographs. All a bit creepy if you ask me!

'What do you know about 'The Joseph Life Care Institute?'

Accordin' to 'arriot *The Joseph'* is the leadin' Research Centre for *'Species Dysphoria'* or *'Species Identity Disorder'* ('SID' for short.) This 'appens when yer 'species identity as a human' fails to match yer 'perceived' or 'desired' identity as another species. Confused? So was I! I thought it were just too silly and far-fetched to be believed, as there's often all kinds of rumours flyin' about. (Even 'arriot was unsure about some of the details 'n' she usually knows everythin'!) Well, I looked *'SID'* up an' wot it means is that people get so un'appy about bein' human that they choose a *'Species Reassignment.'* They really, really want to take on some of the physical and genetic characteristics of an animal they want to become. Yes, that's right – an ANIMAL! To me, wearin' a furry animal suit should be enough (yer can get 'em dead cheap in the summer) but there's no pleasin' some people! From wot I gather, the idea is that anyone wantin' a *'Species Reassignment'* can (for an 'efty fee of course) adopt the full or partial characteristics of any species in the world. Currently, pandas are said to be in vogue. Even level 'eaded 'arriot 'as taken on Lapwing's view that everything is part of the same *'Organic Cosmic Unity.'* This means there's no real difference between the divine and the human, or between men and women or human beings and animals – or even between good and evil and life and death! We (I think meanin' us and animals 'n' everythin') 'ave evolved beyond all that now. As we're all part of *'the One'* (whatever that means) all our differences are just blended into this big 'oneness.' Reminds me of yummy, creamy butter somehow – I digress. The main thing is – you've just to convince yerself 'n' everybody else that there's no differences anymore. Simple eh? If yer think there are real differences then it's you that's at fault! As 'arriot once said, before goin' off to one of 'er *'Spiritual Channelling Meditation'* sessions 'all differences are illusory, *The One'* is the only true reality.' Lor – it gives me an 'eadache just thinkin' about it. It's just all too 'igh falutin' fer the likes o' me.

Another rumour is that there are plans afoot to replenish depleted zoos with 'genetically re-assigned' infants – all in order to boost tourism. Young people 'ave more malleable bodies which makes 'em the best specimens t' use. This explains why 'The Joseph' is willin' to pay surrogate mothers an 'igh price for their children. 'owever, despite the availability of young pre-teen specimens only limited progress 'as been made, especially with non-mammals. Often those 'oo are re-assigned dorn't live long or they come through the process with what 'arriot calls *'unsightly defects.'* One 'appy exception was the take up of jellyfish DNA, which resulted in mountain guides an' divers bein' able to glow a fluorescent green in the dark! Good eh? Such positive measures should make 'The Joseph's' research gain greater public acceptability. I'd love to 'ave my *'ex'* turned into a cow, but come t' think of it she were that anyhow! heh-heh!

'What other challenges have you encountered?'

Well, there's been more trouble wi' the containers again. Finance 'as reduced the size of pre-teen containers to economise on expenses. They came up with some guff about the need to preserve the trees. At first we could 'top 'n' tail 'em just like the way I used to sleep with mah kid brother back in mah old council 'ouse in Swindon. But now we 'ave to squeeze three in an' when yer push 'ard on the lid yer can sometimes 'ear a crunchin' or squelchin' sound. I got on to Lehman Bean about this an' their response was to issue us wi' ear plugs so we wouldn't be distressed by *'unwarranted body noises!'* That was generous of 'em I must say! There's still the smell t' contend with! What we really need are some proper surgical masks, not the flimsy paper things they give us. It's typical of Finance, always wantin' to make savin's at the cost of operations.

'What do I know about the recent Doncaster business?'

Well, we do seem to get one every two or three years – a scandal I mean. Before Doncaster it was 'arringway but this time round Management were more effective in their *'news containment.'* It didn't get out although it was gossiped about during the Supervisor's Conference. T' my knowledge what 'appened was that 'uman cargo 'ad been rented out to a Night Club wantin' a 'Gothic' theme for its 'alloween binge. The team would 'ave got away with it except for the food an' drink stains left on the *'exhibits.'* Morgue staff noticed somethin' was up. Management were told an' the team received what, in that part of the world is called *'a bollocking.'* Luckily it was in no one's interest to *'blab'* about the incident and it was all neatly 'ushed up. I only 'eard about it from this guy I met at the Conference and 'ad to ply 'im with a few drinks before I got the full story. The Night Club owner was let off with a caution – 'e was lucky that there'd been some Councillors attendin' the event so it suited everyone just t' let it go. From what I gather it was the money that talked. Mah contact said they were even plannin' to rent out some o' the cargo to the Gilbert George Gallery in London for a special Day Exhibition on the theme of *'Liquid-Modern Cultural Enlightenment'* – whatever that means. They'd paid a newly redundant undertaker to 'elp 'oo apparently could prevent embarrassin' smells 'n' place the bodies in interestin' poses. Personally, I don't see what's wrong with rentin' out a few 'stiffs' for commercial purposes if no relatives are involved. It would certainly increase our cash flow. Although 'arriot warmly appreciated *'the artistic gestures that were involved,'* the rest o' Senior Management opposed such commercialisation 'on public health grounds.' They're still a little old fashioned and don't want our profession to be *'highly profiled in the public domain.'* Personally, I 'ope the day will come when school parties are taken round as we go about our business – they do this in the Western Provinces or what used to be called the United States and it makes the younger generation a lot more acceptin'. They already accept what used to be called *'euthanasia'* as a perfectly natural and normal thing. 'ere, we've just got round to providin' some sort o' vocational qualification under the title of *'Dispatch Studies.'* In the Western Provinces you can have a full PHD on the subject. What they put into it I just don't know – Lapwing guff I expect.

'What positive developments have happened in connection with your work?'

In the last couple of years our work's gained tremendous acceptability, 'specially amongst the younger generation. Already *'Dispatchin'* is viewed as almost a normal part of everyday life. If you 'ave a medical problem that's not amenable to solution within sixty days you're placed on a 'dispatch data base' an' if there's no improvement after ninety days you're on the trolley. An appeal may delay matters for thirty days but they're expensive and rarely result in anythin'. Personally, I think they're a sop an 'ardly anyone pays for 'em.

'Have personal developments intruded on the job?'

It's funny that you should ask that. Recently, I 'eard from the *'ex.'* 'adn't 'eard a thing fer almost ten years – nor did I want to! Genetic tests 'ad confirmed that 'er first child Danny were indeed mah own an' that I did 'ave some parental responsibility for 'im. *'Oh no,'* I thought, *'she's goin' t' do 'er usual trick of askin' fer money.'* But no not this time – now she sounded desperate an' there was none of 'er usual *'big talk,'* like when she'd 'ad a fling with an old rich banker 'oo liked the funny stuff. But this was somethin' different. She needed me because, 'aving 'ad three children she'd exceeded 'er quota fer single mothers and unless I accepted parentage fer Danny she would 'ave to give up 'er third child for dispatchin' at *'The Joseph Life Care Institute.'* Mah first response 'ad been to tell 'er 'you know the rules – you should live by 'em.' But she pleaded an' reminded me o' the times I used to play football wi' Danny. 'e were a good lad an' it were for 'im that I finally consented. After lettin' 'er sweat for a while, I agreed, on condition she'd be absent whenever I made a parental visit (which I'm obliged to do by law). She agreed to this straight off an' seemed relieved that I'd made it a condition. As usual she spoilt things by askin' for somethin' more. *'Up to 'er old tricks,'* I thought. Now, what she wanted me to do were to take parental rights for Danny's little sister too, even though she wasn't by me but by that banker lover of 'ers. 'er line of argument was that every boy needed a little sister to tease just like I'd 'ad. 'owever, I put mah foot down at this, sayin' I wasn't goin' to take responsibility for another man's child – *"e should do something!"* I'd said. It was then that I learnt the 'ole truth. 'er rich *'sugar daddy'* 'ad got done fer fraud an' 'ad been dispatched when it were decided that most bankers were *'surplus to requirements.'* Also, 'er so called rich banker 'ad taken everythin' she'd 'ad, includin' most o' the money from mah Maintenance Payments. 'ed managed to 'ack into 'er account and 'ad taken it all before tryin' to escape t' Bermuda. ('e left debts totalling quadrillions.) Normally, we'd 'ave ad a boilin' row at this point, but she knew that she 'ad to keep me sweet. I said it was either Danny or nothin'! I mean – what do I care about a child 'oo ain't mine? 'owever, as she usually does, she 'went on and on,' 'ow she couldn't manage 'n' she'd 'ave to sell Cyberella (the little girl) to *'The Joseph.'* To shut 'er up, I said I'd do mah best t' arrange a more 'umane disposal. That's always been the trouble with mah 'ex' – give way to 'er on one thing an' she always wants more. I remember 'ow when Danny was born she'd boasted *'At least I 'ad 'im by a real man!'* (That was at the time she were 'avin' a fling with a bouncer.) She weren't so keen on genetic tests then but I knew Danny were mah own from a family birthmark on 'is back. If 'e weren't mine I wouldn't 'ave tried so 'ard at bein' a good parental operative. Found from 'is report on the Global Cloud that when 'e leaves the Teenage Containment Centre 'e wants to join the Border Defence Force. 'e fancies chasin' an' sinkin' boatloads of unwanted migrants. (They use the term *'Migrant Marine Consignment.'*) 'es a bit of a chip off the old block, 'e is. Must say I'm quite proud of 'im.

Anyway, I 'ad a word with 'arriet about this issue an' she promised that the problem would be promptly sorted – Cyberella would be kept out of *'The Joseph.'* I were relieved – I wouldn't wish any kid to go there – even if it were one of the *'ex's.'* There are better ways to dispatch those *'minors who are deemed a surplus to demographic requirements'* Whoops! Sorry! I'm usin' *'Management speak'* again.

'What are the most pressing current issues?'

Well, in their wisdom Management 'ave decided to replace the containers wi' new plastic stuff. You'd thought they would've learnt from the last time – but no, the *'Crem'* badgered on about *'slow immolation rates.'* This change regardin' containers suggests that a new wave could be on the way. Tests wi' the automated plant on Celtic Island One 'ave begun and there are already encouragin' indications that the neighbourin' fish population is startin' to increase, but there's still an issue with the transport costs. Another sign that somethin' big is up is that 'arriet is t' host a Conference in *'The Old Jail'* to discuss makin', *'atruistic cleansing preparations.'* Such talk always 'appens when somethin' big is in the air. *'The Old Jail'* is judged to 'ave better security facilities in which to discuss 'sensitive matters.' She's called me over (as 'er *'star Supervisor'*) before the Conference to 'elp 'er put the presentation together. She's been in the Western Provinces recently for *'a mixture of personal and professional reasons.'* Doubtless, she'll come back brimmin' with ideas. I just 'ope she doesn't spout too much Lapwing guff. I'll use some earplugs if she does. Apparently, they're both co-authorin' an academic paper on somethin' or other. She gave me the title but I couldn't make out what it said. Oh look, I've got it 'ere – yeah, yeah it's somethin' about *'assisting enlightened users' to 'ascend to a higher level of harmonic union with the transcendent, neo-divine evolutionary force through contacting their inner dolphin!'* All seemed rather fishy to me, ahem!

'Are there any other issues?'

There's just one and that's what to do with the 'Luv Community.' You remember the recent outbreak of the 'Aids3Plus Virus' in our male migrant custodial centres? But perhaps yer don't as they often suffer from such outbreaks (that's why there's talk of replacing human guards with robots). Well, the prisoners didn't matter so much, but it spread to the Security Guards an' would 'ave spread further except for its isolation in South Atlantic, Migrant Custodial Isle 3; as it was, prisoners, staff, 'an even the Governor 'ad to be *'processed'* until their remains were completely vaporised. Our scientific department are already warnin' that it shows signs of mutatin' into the *'Aids4Max version'* which means that it'll be more contagious than the Ebola 3 which caused such a big kafuffle some years back. 'arriot confided to me that the Directors were in *'a ghastly muddle'* as to what to do, 'specially as some were known to 'ave *'certain preferences.'* As an 'olding operation the *'Luv Community'* is bein' put on a *'pink'* rather than a *'red'* alert. This means that they're only bein' considered for a *'partial'* rather than a *'total'* cullin'. That seems reasonable to me as a total cullin' would mean we'd lose some of our best actors and entertainers, not to mention directors too. 'arriot also told me that there's talk in the *'Department of Luv'* of introducin' a licensing system on such relationships. This means they'd be permitted so long as they're proven to be 'clean.' (I can 'ear the cries of *'Luvphobia'* even now!) In the meantime, *'Independent Service Providers'* (*'Rent boys'* they used to be called in my day) will only be allowed to operate within authorised *'Pleasure Centres'* where they'll be subject to medical checks, conducted under police supervision. The last cull resultin' from the 'Aids3Minimum virus' led to such a shortage of personnel that the Global Authorities are keen to preserve those 'oo remain. There's even talk of forcin' some of the unemployed into that sector, but I expect there'll be some resistance. I can vouch for the fact that the *'Personal Service Industry'* prefer volunteers 'oo are less likely to turn nasty on their *'Bodily Service Users.'* 'ow, in this age of financial cutbacks the government is goin' to implement such measures just beats me. Knowin' them I'm sure they'll 'ave a go and we'll 'ave to dispose of the mess as usual. I dunno, we do all this cullin' and we seem no nearer to achievin' this *'ascended humanity'* that Lapwing keeps bangin' on about. To me it's the same old mess every time. Look at me ... do I look ascended with my big belly? Nah! More like <u>ex</u>tended if you ask me!

'Are there any final comments?'

No, the future looks bright and with my personality I 'ope t' strike out 'as a *'Community Dispatch Officer.'* If I get some more qualifications I might even go into *'Technical Consultation,'* which involves assistin' family members to use NEB's to *'cleanly'* dispatch their nearest 'n' dearest. (They will, of course, be charged a hefty fee, with me gettin' some o' the cut.) All this'll involve paperwork an' complyin' wi' Finance's insistence on detailed records. That could create some problems fer me, but overall though, I'm 'ighly optimistic about the future wi' the Dignity Dispatch Service. Things will become clearer when I've seen 'arriet at that pre-conference meetin' tomorrow. One day I'm sure she'll 'ave me an' I can't wait fer it, but I mustn't allow the personal to intrude on the professional. *'Somethin' is about to blow'* as we say in our business and I can't wait to see what it is.

With the self-administered interview now over Kenny disconnects the microphone lead from the recorder and places both in the dresser's top drawer. He then turns around and glances fondly at the teddy bear before exclaiming, "She'll like that!" He nods to a switch and the light fades. Darkness is complete, except for the tiniest of lights emanating from the Nano Fly's infra-red eyes that are still trained on his every move.

IN-HOUSE DISPATCH NOTE	
Job Title:	Unit Supervisor 101
Name:	Kenneth England (known as *'Kenny'*)
Age:	56 **Gender:** Genetic Male
Next of Kin:	A son, Danny (not in contact)
Dispatch Date:	31st October
Dispatch Location:	Waiting room, Major Unit 3 *'The Old Jail'*
Dispatch Method:	A trial *'Nano'* dart, shot from the security camera
Outcome:	Satisfactory, despite some minor convulsions
Reason for Dispatch:	To reduce redundancy costs
Follow Up Action:	Unit to be used for training purposes only, all remaining operatives to be dispatched
Rationale:	Replacement by the new automated facilities on Celtic Island One
Dispatch Proposers:	
First Proposed by: **Seconded by:**	Harriet Lapwing (Human Resources Director) Lehman Bean (Financial Director)
Authorised by:	Dr Galton (*'Lord Galton of Down'*)
Records:	Edited versions of the interviews with the Recruitment Section are to be archived. Despite some personal indiscretions they convey a highly positive image of the organization and might be of value to researchers studying its invaluable work on behalf of humanity.
Means of Disposal:	Nano-Consumption
Claimants:	Remains claimed by Harriot Lapwing *'for ornamental purposes'*
Further Comments:	*Gone but not forgotten my darling mentor! You were great fun to be with, if a trifle indiscreet. You will look most fetching in the nice new Chinese Urn I had prepared for you on my mantelpiece, alongside my other exhibits. I promise to get Lapwing to dust it every day. Thanks again for the lovely teddy bear, I've named it after you, xxx Harriet*

Afterward

'The Exit Machine' was written in the conviction that the present campaign (2012) to legalise assisted suicide and euthanasia could be laying the foundation for a mass extermination society. It mirrors the earlier euthanasia campaign of pre-war Germany (1919-1939) and what happened there, is I believe, beginning to happen here through a well crafted but fundamentally dishonest campaign to legalise assisted dying. Present within Britain is the same toxic mix of cultural decadence, economic instability, political corruption and ideological extremism which characterized Weimar Germany (1919-1933) and led to the rise of Hitler (Rees 1997 & Sturmer 1999). Equally present is a similar weakening in democratic processes and a growing anti-Semitism from both the political right and left. In September 2008 the Western World came close to suffering another *'Great Depression'* which would have served to reinforce already existing financial pressures to remove those deemed *'a burden upon society.'* As the historical explorations of Laurence Rees (1997) and Niall Fergurson (2011) demonstrated, horrors like Auschwitz and Treblinka didn't emerge from nowhere. There was a long and surreptitious build up; first in German South West Africa (in 1904), then through the dehumanizing experience of the First World War (1914-1918) and the economic hardships that followed. Throughout all of these upheavals there was a steady loss of respect for human life (as shown by the growing violence throughout this period). Lending intellectual respectability to this *'dehumanizing'* development was the Darwinian-based *'Eugenics Movement'* which believed in improving the genetic profile of the population through selective breeding. (Its long term aim was to enhance the process of human evolution in order to create a perfect *'master race.'*) By the 1930's, compulsory sterilization and the murder of those with hereditary defects had become acceptable in Germany – not least amongst the eugenics-influenced medical profession. However, the first killings were conducted secretly in order to avoid public opposition and to *'test out'* new disposal methods. The techniques used in the Nazi euthanasia program were (along with key personnel) transferred to the

concentration camp system. These initial inroads provided an infrastructure and skills-base in which murder on an industrial scale could take place. Present was a typical pattern of historical change in which a slow build up (over the course of three to four decades) was followed by a massive escalation within a shorter span of several years. There's every reason to believe that such a pattern could be repeated, particularly if (as seems likely) economic and financial pressures upon the Welfare State continue to increase. Another *'Great Depression'* could see the rapid introduction of a mass extermination society. By lending respectability to *'assisted dying'* pro-euthanasia groups like *'Dignatas'* and *'Exit'* have already created a climate of opinion in which such a development would be welcomed. Like the earlier *'Eugenics Movement'* they've helped make the unacceptable acceptable. Truly, *'there's nothing new under the sun,'* (Ecclesiastes 1:9).

When it came to the *'knocking off'* of unwanted members of society the Nazis were at least more honest than today's generation of would-be mass exterminators. From the very beginning their propaganda had made it clear that financial considerations were an important factor in driving their program. One poster, showing a sinister looking *'mental defective'* was accompanied by a caption which read; *"This person, suffering from hereditary defects, costs the community 60,000 Reichmarks during his lifetime. Fellow German, that is your money too,"* (http://en.wikipedia.org/wiki/Eugenics Retrieved, Thursday, 19/5/2011).

In contrast, today's advocates of *'assisted dying,'* like Tallis (2011) make much play on such misleading euphemisms as *'death with dignity'* and the use of positive sounding words like *'humane'* or *'compassion.'* In reality, the whole business of *'assisted dying'* would quickly degenerate into a matter of budget cutbacks and savings targets. A bankrupt government would welcome any measure to reduce welfare spending. A Darwinian situation would be allowed to take its course in which the fittest would conspire to eliminate the less fit in order to secure the former's survival and prosperity. No mercy would be shown to the weak who instead, would be dehumanised and viewed as disposable consumer products.

Arguments presented by pro-euthanasia pressure groups tend to be characterized by a high degree of emotionalism and also by a self-interested naivety. Conveniently overlooked in the case they put forward is the fact that, once officially sanctioned organizational structures are set up, they will (like empire-building bureaucracies everywhere) seek to expand their remit to eliminate those labelled as a burden upon society. Inevitably, they will acquire a momentum of their own and controls designed to provide safeguards against abuse will become ineffective (as already proven in notorious child abuse cases). They will also seek to expand their operations into hitherto unrelated areas. In such circumstances, what had initially been a cottage industry of *'assisted dying'* could quickly develop into a mass industry of compulsory extermination. Any legislation favouring assisted suicide or euthanasia begs the two-part question, *'What kind of structures will be set up to implement that legislation?'* and *'What agendas will senior members of those structures come to pursue?'*

The mainstream media has largely failed to raise such questions in debates over assisted dying. This suggests either a high degree of journalistic incompetence or an equally high degree of complicity. In reality, the argument for legalising assisted suicide is deeply flawed. Any such legislation could easily have lethal, unintended and far-reaching consequences.

Perhaps the most devastating question to ask the pro-euthanasia lobby is *'Who will do the killing?'* To put it crudely *'Who'll knock off the unwanted?'* Only three alternatives are possible and against each a valid and serious objection can be raised – as outlined in the following question **(Q)** and answer **(A)** format: -

Q1: Will it be the *'next of kin?'*

A1: No – it would be too distressing an event for them. Also, they may well be too easily swayed by altruistic emotional or ulterior financial motives to *'do the job'* in a professional and dignified manner. Huge feelings of guilt may well be a long term legacy.

Q2: Should it be the medical profession?

A2: No – the widespread practice of *'mercy killing'* would lead to a subtle change in the mental attitude of medical staff and result in Doctors violating the Hippocratic Oath. It could well result in the *'Shipmanization'* of the medical profession i.e. converting it into a <u>life taking</u> rather than a <u>life preserving</u> body.

Q3: What about entrusting a *'Specialist Unit'* with the task?

A3: No – such a *'Unit'* would have the potential to attract rather unpleasant people with homicidal inclinations. Also, once established, it could well acquire its own self-perpetuating momentum and be extremely difficult to control.

Each of the above three answers offer little encouragement to those advocating a *'pro-euthanasia'* stance; any one of them could easily create structures of abuse, thereby having an injurious effect upon society. Present is the practical tri-dilemma of the pro-euthanasia case. Again, these are issues which should have been raised by the media. One wonders when journalists will show some competence in handling this crucial subject. They need to point out that the case for *'assisted dying'* founders on the central question; *'Who will do the killing?'*

At this point, it's appropriate to heed the warning given by Suzanne Evans (2007) in an exceleeant and thought provoking book entitled *'Hitler's Forgotten Victims: The Holocaust and the Disabled'* (Tempus Publishing Ltd   ISBN: 978-0-7524-4175-7)   she wrote exploring Hitler's murder of up to 750,000 disabled people. *'The conditions that made the Nazi regime's murderous programs possible – apathy when confronted with affronts to human dignity, the presence of a charismatic leader who devalues and dehumanizes anyone different, negative attitudes and stereotypes about people with disabilities and the manipulation of science and technology to achieve unthinkable goals – persist today in many parts of the world. We thus cannot assume that the atrocities the Nazis committed against the disability community were a unique event, never to be repeated. Our own self-interest as well as our obligation requires us to continue to explore and remember these events and the conditions in which they occurred,"* (Evans 2007, pp.164-5).

My own reckoning is that the Western World is only one economic depression away from constructing a mass extermination society. This will have a major negative impact upon the disabled (and other vulnerable groups too). Should such a depression occur this type of society will quickly emerge within a period of several years, because the cultural and technical framework it needs is already firmly in place. Moreover, recent history (including the UK riots of August 2011) has demonstrated how advanced societies can, under the pressure of adverse events, easily lapse into a mixture of mob lawlessness and systematic cruelty. There's every reason to believe that such a lapse could take place on a large scale in today's Western World. Should such a mass extermination society come into being each one of us could become a potential target. Once the momentum for industrialised mass murder has been generated it's often very difficult to stop it in its tracks. If the present trends toward dehumanisation remain prevalent throughout western society they will produce horrors equal to anything seen at the Auschwitz-Birkenau death camp. Only this time it will be with a technology far in advance of anything the Nazis ever had.

Whilst making this observation, I have in mind the faces of those adult students with head injuries with whom it's been a great privilege to teach the history of Western Civilization. As more emotive pro-euthanasia propaganda was being churned out through the media I looked at my class and thought *'people like you are going to be targets. Something will have to be done.'* I also had the same sentiment when looking at those with mental health difficulties in some of the cultural circles in which I've mixed. It's been for their sake especially that I've produced *'The Exit Machine.'*

FURTHER READING

B1) Booklist

B1.1: On the Collapse of Western Civilization

Atwood Margaret (2010)
The Handmaid's Tale
Vintage Classics
ISBN: 978-0099511663

Barzun Jacques (2000)
From Dawn to Decadence:
500 Years of Western Cultural Life
Harper-Collins Publishers
ISBN: 0-06-017586-9

Brierley Peter Dr (2000)
The Tide Is Running Out
Christian Research
ISBN: 1-85321-137-0

Brierley Peter Dr (2006)
Pulling Out Of the Nosedive:
A Contemporary Picture of Churchgoing:
What the 2005 English Church Census Reveals
Christian Research
ISBN: 1-85321-168-3

Brown G. Callum (2001)
The Death of Christian Britain
Routledge
ISBN: 0-415-284-7

Bruce Steve (2002)
God Is Dead:
Secularisation in the West
Blackwell Publishing
ISBN: 0-631-23275-3

Campbell Colin (2007)
The Easternisation of the West:
A Thematic Cultural Change in the Modern Age
Paradigm Publishers
ISBN: 978-1-59451-224-7

Ferguson Niall (2011)
Civilization: The West and the Rest
Allen Lane
ISBN: 978-1-846-14273-4

Galbraith Kenneth John (1953 - penguin edition 1992)
The Great Crash of 1929
Penguin
ISBN: 978-0-14-013609-8

Hitchens Peter (2009)
The Broken Compass:
How British Politics Lost its Way
Continuum
ISBN: 978-1-84706-405-9

Huxley Aldous (2007)
Brave New World
Vintage Books
ISBN: 978-0099518471

Moreton Cole (2010)
Is God Still An Englishman?
How We Lost Our Faith
(But Found New Soul)
Little Brown
ISBN: 978-1-4087-0180-5

Orwell George (2004)
1984
Penguin Classics
ISBN: 978-0141187761

Phillips Melanie (2010)
The World Turned Upside Down:
The Global Battle over God, Truth, and Power
Encounter Books
ISBN: 978-1-59403-375-9 486

Thomas M. D. (1998)
Alexander Solzhenitsyn:
A Century in his life
Abacus
ISBN: 0-349-11115-4

Williams Rowan (2002)
The Poems of Rowan Williams
Perpetua Press
ISBN: 1-870882-16-4

Zimbardo Philip (2007)
The Lucifer Effect:
How Good People Turn Evil
Rider ISBN: 978-1-84-413577-6

B1.2: On Weimar Germany and Nazism

Bonhoeffer Dietrich (1978)
Life together
SCM
ISBN: 334-00904-9

Evans E. Suzanne (2007)
Hitler's Forgotten Victims:
The Holocaust and the Disabled
Tempus Publishing Ltd
ISBN: 978-0-7524-4175-7

Fitzgibbon Constantine – Translator (2000)
Commandment of Auschwitz:
The Autobiography of Rudolf Hoess
Phoenix
ISBN: 978-1-84212-024-8

Heschel Susannah (2008)
The Aryan Jesus:
Christian Theologians and the Bible in Nazi Germany
Princeton University Press
ISBN13: 978-0-691-12531-2

Maser Werner (1971)
Hitler: Legend, Myth and Reality
Harper & Row

Rees Laurence (1997)
The Nazis:
A Warning from History
BBC
ISBN: 0-563-38704

Robertson Edwin (1987)
The Shame and the Sacrifice:
The Life and Preaching of Dietrich Bonhoeffer
Hodder and Stoughton
ISBN: 0-340-41063-9

Sturmer Michael (1999)
The German Century
Weidenfeld & Nicolson
ISBN: 0-2978-2524-0

B2) Articles

Adams Stephen (2012)
Killing babies no different from abortion, experts say
Parents should be allowed to have their newborn babies killed because they are
"morally irrelevant" and ending their lives is no different to abortion, a group of
medical ethicists linked to Oxford University has argued.
Telegaph.co.uk Wednesday, 29th February 2012

Cook Michael (2011)
Where Is The Worst Place In The World To Be A Doctor?
MercatorNet Wednesday, 21st September 2011

Connolly Kate (2012)
Dutch mobile euthanasia units to make house calls:
New scheme called 'Life End' will respond to sick people whose own doctors have
refused to help them end their lives at home
Guardian.co.uk Thursday, 1st March 2012

Giubilini Alberto and Minerva Francesca (2012)
After-birth abortion: why should the baby live?
JME Online First, published on Friday, 2nd March 2012 as
10.1136/medethics-2011-10041

Kelly Tom and Fagge Nick (2011)
Dr Death Suicide Film Being Shown In Schools: Euthanasia Fanatic Gives Workshop On How to Kill Yourself in Educational Video for 14-Year-Olds
Daily Mail Saturday, 16th April 2011

Lawson Dominic (2012)
Money – Not Morals – Fuels the Suicide Lobby
Sunday Times 8th January 2012 p.1.20
Macrae Fiona (2012)
Doctors 'should have the right to KILL unwanted or disabled babies at birth as they are not a real person' claims former Oxford academic
Dailymail.co.uk Thursday, 1st March 2012

Muggeridge Malcolm (1966)
The Great Liberal Death Wish
New Statesman, 11th March 1966
(For replies to Muggeridge's article please refer to the Letter Column of the New Statesman Friday, 18th March 1966)

Tallis Raymond (2011)
The Scandal of Doctors against Assisted Dying
The Times Tuesday 11th October 2011

Thomas Liz (2011)
BBC Accused of Being 'Cheerleader for Assisted Suicide' After Filming Man Killing Himself in Terry Pratchett Documentary
Daily Mail Friday, 15th April 2011

B3) Web Sites

http://blogs.bmj.com/medical-ethics/2012/02/28/liberals-are-disgusting-in-defence-of-the-publication-of-after-birth-abortion/
(Retrieved Wednesday, 7/3/2012)

http://en.wikipedia.org/wiki/Eugenics
(Retrieved, Thursday, 19/5/2011)

http://en.wikipedia.org/wiki/Julian_Savulescu
(Retrieved Wednesday, 7/3/2012)

http://jme.bmj.com/content/early/2012/03/01/medethics-2011-100411.abstract#aff-1
(Retrieved Wednesday, 7/3/2012)

http://jme.bmj.com/content/early/2012/03/01/medethics-2011-100411.full.pdf+html
(Retrieved Wednesday, 7/3/2012)

http://www.dailymail.co.uk/news/article-1377062/BBC-accused-cheerleader-assisted-suicide-Terry-Pratchett-documentary.html#ixzz1ZCF2fNTq
(Retrieved Monday, 18/4/2011)

http://www.dailymail.co.uk/news/article-1377412/Dr-Philip-Nitschke-gives-euthanasia-workshop-video-14-year-olds.html#ixzz1ZCDAQOua
(Retrieved Monday, 18/4/2011)

http://www.dailymail.co.uk/news/article-2108433/Doctors-right-kill-unwanted-disabled-babies-birth-real-person-claims-Oxford-academic.html?printingPage=true
(Retrieved Wednesday, 7/3/2012)

http://www.guardian.co.uk/world/2012/mar/01/dutch-mobile-euthanasia-units
(Retrieved Thursday, 22/3/2012)

http://www.mercatornet.com/articles/view/where_is_the_worst_place_in_the_world_to_be_a_doctor
(Retrieved Wednesday, 21/9/2011)

http://www.telegraph.co.uk/health/healthnews/9113394/Killing-babies-no-different-from-abortion-experts-say.html
(Retrieved Wednesday, 7/3/2012)

http://www.theblaze.com/stories/yes-we-are-serious-ethicists-defend-after-birth-abortion-argument-in-raucous-radio-interview/
(Retrieved Thursday, 22/3/2012)

B4) Television Programmes

Prachett Terry
Choosing To Die
BBC2 Broadcast on Monday, 13th June 2011 from 9.00-10.00 pm

Choosing to Die Debate
BBC2 Broadcast on Monday, 13th June 2011 from 10.00-10.30 pm

Notes

www.ingramcontent.com/pod-product-compliance
Lightning Source LLC
Chambersburg PA
CBHW021131130626
46554CB00002B/957